W9-CKU-782

Only Girls Allowed

Only Girls Allowed

THE PINK LOCKER SOCIETY

Debra Moffitt

ST. MARTIN'S GRIFFIN

NEW YORK

www.stmartins.com

Chapter Illustrations copyright © Chuck Gonzales

Library of Congress Cataloging-in-Publication Data

Moffitt, Debra.
    Only girls allowed / Debra Moffitt.—1st ed.
        p. cm.
    Summary: Thirteen-year-old Jemma, her best friends Kate and Piper, and new student Bet are invited to join a secret society at school meant to help other girls with their problems, but membership brings many complications.
    ISBN 978-0-312-64502-1
    [1. Secret societies—Fiction.   2. Best friends—Fiction.
3. Friendship—Fiction.   4. Middle schools—Fiction.   5. Schools—Fiction.]   I. Title.
    PZ7.M7245Onl 2010
    [Fic]—dc22

                                                    2010022068

First published in the United States by The Nemours Foundation/KidsHealth

First St. Martin's Griffin Edition: September 2010

Printed in August 2010 in the United States of America by RR Donnelly, Harrisburg, Virginia.

10   9   8   7   6   5   4   3   2   1

One

For one and only one day of the school year, I am so excited that my body works as its own alarm clock. Waaaaaaaay early in the morning, my eyes pop open. I wake up in my quiet room, with my cat purring on top of the covers and sun streaking through the window. My clothes are clean and ready, waiting for me on a hanger on my bedroom doorknob. Socks are tucked inside the shoes I'll wear. My lunch is in the fridge, and my backpack is loaded with new pens, pencils, folders, and even a few "supplies" in case my you-know-what shows up at school.

I know from experience that I will not wake up so chipmunk chipper on the 179 school days that will follow this one. On those days, my bed holds me down like a magnet and I simply can't-can't-can't move. And I don't move until my mom calls me for the third time, when her voice gets that "Jemma, I'm not foolin' around here" sound. But today, she doesn't have to call at all. I'm not tired. I'm wired. I could run a marathon or bake a cake before the bus comes. Energy runs through my body and sparks up and down each strand of my wavy blond hair. I want eighth grade to start, and start now.

BEEP! I dig through my already-packed backpack for my phone. It's a text message from my best friend, Kate.

KATE: Forrest alert!
That means she's already on the bus and she's spotted him. THE Forrest McCann.
ME: wearing?
KATE: camo shorts w/ blue t
ME: sigh . . .

Who wouldn't want eighth grade to start right away? Eighth grade is what I call one of the "royal" grades. There are three of them. The core royal grades are fifth grade, eighth grade, and twelfth grade. Get the connection? Royal grades are when you're in the top grade at your school. In other words, you get to be queens (and kings) and rule the school that year. The top-top-tippy top would be twelfth grade—the senior year of high school, with the prom and driving cars and all of that. But I know eighth is gonna be magic, too.

Ask an old person (like a parent), and they'll probably say there's not much difference between the first day of sixth grade and the first day of eighth. OK, it is true that any sixth grade girl at my school, Margaret Simon Middle, will . . .

1. Eat breakfast.
2. Get dressed.
3. Fix her hair.
4. Grab her backpack.
5. Hop on the bus.
6. Look for her friends.
7. Go to homeroom.
8. Open her new locker and move in.
9. Hope for the best.

But look more closely at the sixth-grade girl and the eighth-grade girl. Their first days of school are as different as Alaska and Hawaii. I should know. I've visited both—the states and the grades. The sixth grader doesn't yet know that at Margaret Simon, headbands are in and barrettes are out. She doesn't know that you need to pick a spot *before* the first day of school to meet your friends in the lobby or you'll never find them in the crowd.

Our 6GG (sixth-grade girl) doesn't know to sling her backpack over only one shoulder. And unless she's what my mother calls an "early bloomer," she doesn't know that over both shoulders she needs a B-R-A. Even if you're Flatty McFlat Chest, like me, you still wear a bra. It's part of the uniform.

The 6GG will fumble and fuss with her new locker, remembering the good old days when she just stowed everything in her desk. The lockers at Margaret Simon are sea-foam green on the outside, big enough to stand up in, and the combination lock is built into the door, like a bank safe. So there our girl will stand, clutching a slip of paper with the combination written on it, backpack hanging from both shoulders, and two pancakes flying free under her shirt. The locker won't open on the first try, or the second, making the first day of sixth grade feel as bone-cold and lonely as Prospect Creek, Alaska, before sunrise.

But if you're in eighth grade, like me, you know the rules of the school. Today, a hot and steamy August morning, my headband is in place. The bra is on board. My backpack is hooked to only one shoulder. My two best friends and I had decided to meet where we always do—at the water fountain near the auditorium doors. In fact, we had even specified that if that area was too crowded (or if Taylor Mayweather was doing one of her MSTV broadcasts there), we'd meet next to the vending machine instead.

And when it comes to my locker, no sweat. I calmly head to the number they assigned me (2121) in the eighth-grade locker block. I approach my new home, already armed with a little shelf to organize my space, a mirror so I can check my teeth for food particles after lunch, photos I want to stick on the door, and even tape to get them stuck. I spin the dial of the combination lock, feeling as tropical and sunny as it is outside. And I could dance the hula after I hear the *chunka-chunk* that tells me I got the combination just right—on the first try, too. Aloha, eighth grade!

But that's where this story gets kind of funny. Not "someone dropped their tray in the cafeteria" funny, but funny-strange. My mother once told me that there are certain days that you just know are going to change your life. Like the day you start college or the day you get married. From that point on, she said, you know lots and lots of stuff is going to change. And you'll have this new dividing line in your life—with everything that happened before on one side and everything new on the other. My mom is always saying stuff like this. (If your mother is also a poet, you know what I mean.)

"Don't worry," I told Mom, "I can't go to college for another five years, and nobody has asked me to marry them." (This was almost true.)

"And," she said, "there are other days that are just as life changing, but you don't see them coming. Life can surprise you."

Today was one of those days.

Two

O K. I didn't hula dance in front of my locker, but I did swing the door wide open in a ta-dah! kind of way. I almost whacked Clementine Caritas, my locker neighbor to the left.

"Jeez, watch it!" she said, blocking the door with her perfectly manicured, shiny red nails.

"Oops. Sorry!"

Clementine was not a friend. She was the real deal—a teen model who had photo shoots in New York, Los Angeles, and on little islands that I'd never heard of. Clem wasn't pretty in the cutesy blond way that Taylor Mayweather was. Her face was all big gray eyes and sharp angles—a high and wide forehead, strong nose, and jutting cheekbones.

As awkward as it was nearly bashing the precious head of a teen model, I was glad my locker door didn't swing open the other way. If it did, I might have hit Forrest. That he was my locker neighbor to the right was another reason to hula. I had a whole year of opportunities to say *hi* to the absolute hottest guy in school. That is, if I could look at him and form the word *hi* without passing out first. I've had other crushes, but none like this one. It's a mystery to me why he still flutters my heart, when we've known each other for more than ten years and our moms are friends.

Oh, yeah, did I mention he was Taylor Mayweather's boyfriend? I wonder what she would think if she knew Forrest was my "line partner" in preschool? Seriously! When we were four, we had to hold hands all the time. Taylor didn't arrive on the scene until fifth grade, and I still haven't forgiven her for what happened that year. I'll tell you this much: It involved me, a slumber party, and a bowl of warm water.

My new locker let out a breath of cool air, and I stood for a minute to enjoy its emptiness, like a brand-new apartment all my own. So many possibilities. My mind was buzzing with all the organizing and arranging I wanted to do. But before I could reach for a roll of tape to start putting up my favorite pix, I saw it. On the back wall of my locker, staring right at me—it was the front door to another locker.

This one was hot pink and shiny. Attached to the pink door was a note:

Shhh!
You are now a member of the Pink Locker Society.
More details to come.
Shhhhh!

Remember that stuff about the dividing line in life? Draw mine here. I inhaled a short, sharp breath, dropped my armload of books, and slammed the door. I even thought about leaning against it the way they do in cartoons. Was somebody in there? Should I have opened that pink door? Was this a joke? All my stuff lay in a heap while everyone else busied themselves with interior locker design.

Clem looked at me coolly. If she wasn't such an ice princess, I might have pulled her down to my height and showed her the inside of my locker. Instead, I collected myself and looked away as though everything were fine. As for Forrest, he didn't notice me (big surprise) or my gasp. I tore around the block of lockers, looking for someone I could tell.

Three

n o surprise who I was looking for—Kate (BFF1) and Piper (BFF2). I turned left, and since everyone still had their heads in their lockers, I started scanning the backs of heads for Piper's auburn ponytail and Kate's brown braid. Nothing. I turned the next corner and found them both. They were standing close together, almost touching, as they stared into a locker. They looked like they were studying a painting at an art museum.

"Guys!" I gasped, a little out of breath. But they only made eye contact with me for an instant, before turning back to the locker.

"I just . . . (pant) found something crazy in . . . (pant) my locker."

This time, they looked up and locked eyes with me.

They said nothing, but they parted so I could step in between. We bunched close, the three of us, like flowers on the same stem. All six eyes saw the same thing—a shiny pink locker door. Same note, too.

I felt hot and woozy, the way I sometimes did before a test, or when Forrest brushed by me. I looked around and didn't see anyone else standing around in amazement. Some were still taping and stacking, but most seemed to be finished with their locker work and were beginning to head down the eighth-grade hallway.

"There's one in Kate's locker, too," Piper said. "I'm opening mine."

"No way!" I said, pulling her back by her shoulder. "It says 'More details to come.' We have to wait."

"And it says 'Shhh!' too."

"But it does *not* say 'Do not open,'" Piper said, "so I'm opening it."

She looked like she was feeling for something under a bed. I heard her tug on a metal latch, but it wouldn't open.

"It's locked," Piper said.

"No duh. It's a lock-er," Kate said. "You need the combination."

Piper stuck her head way inside the locker, popped back out again, and said, "This lock has letters on it instead of numbers."

Just as I was about to have a look for myself, the bell rang for first period. People scattered. Piper shrugged and

Kate walked toward her locker. I rounded the corner and saw my stuff still in a heap. I quickly turned the combo on my locker. *Chunka-chunk.* It opened. Without looking, I threw my stuff inside and went to class.

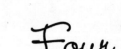

Four

For a few days, we didn't know what to do. Piper kept tugging on the pink locker door, but it was always locked. Kate Googled the Pink Locker Society and found something in the archives at our local university, where her dad works. Trouble was, you needed a password to see it. And me, well, I pretty much tried to avoid my locker. When I absolutely had to open it to get something, I acted like there was a hungry beast asleep inside. I was very quiet and pulled my books out gently. I closed the door firmly but never slammed it.

Aside from discovering the pink locker, eighth grade wasn't starting out all that magically. I didn't understand geometry; Forrest had not said so much as *hi* to me despite thirteen locker encounters; and I still hadn't gotten my you-know-what. On the bright side, the new gym teacher was nice and said, after we ran a lap, that I should consider going out for track.

Did you know *aloha* means more than one thing? It's hello, good-bye, and a whole bunch of other stuff. It's even a technical term that has to do with sending radio and satellite messages. So what did I mean when I said aloha to eighth grade?" I meant hello, bring it on, let's chow down at the buffet of exciting times in store for me, Jemma.

Eighth grade was my chance (finally!) to be popular. Not Taylor Mayweather or Forrest McCann popular—and definitely not as popular as Clementine Caritas. But I wanted the easy-peasy popularity that just about every eighth-grader gets to have just by being one of the oldest kids at school. We are owed it. But how popular can you be when you're me—the only girl in eighth grade who's afraid of her locker?

Five

On Thursday, the "Shhh!" note in my locker was replaced by a new one. It was printed on pretty pink stationery, and the lettering was fancy, like a wedding invitation. It said:

First meeting of the Pink Locker Society
Friday at 1:35 P.M.
To open your pink locker, use the following letter
combination: S-E-R-V-E. This combination will be
*activated **only** from 1:35 P.M. to 1:36 P.M.*
The meeting begins five minutes after the start of the
study-hall period. You have been excused from study hall.
*Enter through your **own** pink locker door! If too many girls are*
climbing through the same locker, it attracts attention.

We looked at each other, then back to the locker, and at each other again.

"We have to go *through* the locker door? Through to where?" I asked.

Nobody answered, but Piper smiled widely. "This is unbelievably cool. It's like Harry Potter or something."

"But Margaret Simon isn't Hogwarts," said Kate. "We're *normal* girls. It's not like we can do magic or something."

"Not yet . . . ," Piper said, flicking her pencil at me like a magic wand.

I grabbed her pencil and gave her an exasperated look. "Nobody is doing any magic. I don't know about you guys, but I'm not going in there tomorrow. Notice how it doesn't say anything about when the meeting is *over*? We could be stuck in there forever!"

Kate pointed out that the note said we were excused from study hall, so it sounded like we'd be out at 2:10 for our next class. Sometimes Kate was cautious like me, but not this time. She was going. And Piper couldn't be stopped.

"I'm not saying I'm not nervous, but I think we should go," Kate said. "It really is an honor."

"What do you know about it, Kate?" I snapped. "We don't even know what the Pink Locker Society is."

"I know a little," Kate said. "All I can say is that I know it's a good thing."

Six

id you ever have a friend who always reads every little instruction on the inside of the board-game box? The friend who already knows how to play but reads the directions every time to improve her grasp of each little rule? If you're not properly spinning the spinner or discarding your cards the right way or adding up how much the bank owes you, this girl will let you know. That girl is me.

I like rules. Piper could care less what the rules are. And Kate falls somewhere in the middle, which is good because she keeps Piper and me from having a billion arguments. So far there were no rules for the Pink Locker Society other than to be there the next day at exactly 1:35 P.M.

That night on the phone, I tried to squeeze more information out of Kate about the PLS, but she wasn't talking.

"I can't say," Kate said. "Just show up tomorrow at 1:35. I'm bringing my camera."

Seven

For the first time in recorded history, the school day was going fast. Too fast. Before I knew it, I had finished lunch and we were just one period away from the Pink Locker Society meeting. I really wanted to know how we had been excused from study hall. What if it wasn't true? Did I really want to get detention for skipping class?

Math flew by like it's never flown before. I never thought I'd ache for another parabola, but I was disappointed when Mr. Ford said that was all for today. He told us to use our first study hall of the year wisely.

"How you spend your daily study hall can very well determine the course of your entire school year," he said.

You don't know how right you are, Mr. Ford.

I stopped in the girls' bathroom after class and waited

until 1:33, giving myself a minute to get to my locker and a minute to unlock that funky letters-instead-of-numbers code. S-E-R-V-E. Serve who? Or as Mom would correct me, Serve whom?

The eighth grade locker block was actually a "U." Piper, Kate, and I were on three different sides of the "U." My locker was in the middle on the east side, facing the bathrooms; Piper's was in the middle of the west side, near the windows; and Kate's was in the middle of the south side, at the bottom of the "U" near the stairwell. In the long days until today, we wondered if that meant something. If you had looked at it from an aerial photo, we formed a sort of triangle.

At 1:34, I stood in front of my locker practically alone. Everyone else had moved along to study hall or their next class. I pretended to be looking for something until the last straggler left. My face felt funny—quivery—as I examined the combination lock. The alphabet circled the dial.

1:35! I took the dial between my thumb and pointer finger and started spelling. S-E-. . . . This was harder than I thought. Once I put my head in the locker, it blocked most of the light. I found R. . . . Now where was V? Earlier, I did the math to determine how many seconds I had per letter—twelve. I thought that was more than enough, but it wasn't when the clock was ticking. Suddenly, I had big floppy clown hands and I couldn't see. Finally, I found the V. Now on to E. . . .

Ugh! I went past it! Now, I had to start over. *Breathe*, I told myself. *Don't panic.* S-E-R . . . I heard voices from behind my pink locker door—the other girls were already in. . . .

"Miss Colwin," a voice called from the real-locker side of the world. It was Mr. Ford.

"Is everything all right?"

I spun around, blocking his view of the pink door.

"I'm fine. Good. Great. Thanks. Just looking for something. Going to get a jump on that extra credit you just gave out."

"Okay," he said. "Please get moving to study hall, Jemma."

"On my way!"

I turned around and waited for the sound of him walking away. The pink locker remained shut. I had to start over again and it was now too late. 1:37. Ugh! I had missed my chance. I tried the combination again, but the locker wouldn't budge. I sat down, my back to the pink, and wondered what to do next. I was angry at myself but relieved I didn't have to go in. But I was also worried about (and maybe a little jealous of) my friends.

I felt left out in the same way that I did at the amusement park last summer when everyone else went on the roller coaster. Nothing to do but shuffle my feet until their ride was over and they came spilling down the exit ramp, all laughs and smiles. I pulled out my class schedule and tried to see where my study hall room was. But the computer-generated schedule was no help. Instead of a room number, it said ***. I couldn't go to study hall even if I wanted to.

It was then that I heard a rustling noise behind me. A moment later, Kate opened my pink locker door. It abruptly swung in instead of out and she pulled me in by my forearm.

She whisper-yelled to me, "Watch the step, watch the step!" but it was too late. It was one of those steps that's three or four inches steeper than it should be and throws you off completely. I was in, but I was down on one knee, like I was waiting for someone to say, "On your mark, get set, go!"

Kate pulled me up, reached in to close my real locker door, then closed the pink one behind her. I saw that in her other hand she had her camera. I was very glad she hadn't thought to take a photo of me at this unflattering moment.

Piper dusted me off for dramatic effect and said, "Have a nice trip?"

I wanted to say something clever, but my brain was too busy taking it all in. Kate was doing the same, snapping photos of every angle of the place. We were in what looked like a super-rich old lady's house. My knee hardly hurt because I had fallen onto a soft rose-colored rug with fringe on the ends. There was a living room area filled with formal furniture, needlepoint pillows, lamps with glass domes over them, and lace doilies on the tables. Big sections of the rest of the room were closed off by thick plastic tarps. The place was clearly under construction, and there was a fine coating of dust on a long table, where twelve people could have sat comfortably for dinner.

A large, boxy pink telephone sat in the center of the table. The earpiece was attached to the phone with a twisty cord, and instead of push buttons, it had a spinny thing, like the phones in old movies. The phone was tethered to a big silver speaker.

Oddly, someone had left us snacks—fresh fruit salad and a glass pitcher of lemonade. A short flight of wooden stairs led to a loft, where I discovered four desks with machines on top of them. Were they sewing machines? I should've worn my glasses.

"I hope they're going to renovate the bathroom next, because it could use an update," Piper told us, pointing over her shoulder at a closed door. Her mother was a real estate agent, so she knew a lot about the finer touches in bathrooms these days, like granite countertops, dual showers, and soaking tubs. "Very vintage stuff in there. But at least the toilet works."

"See, I told you this would be good," Kate said, pinching my arm.

I thought about how people say "pinch me" when they're dreaming. Kate pinched me and I didn't wake up. We were at school, somehow inside the eighth-grade locker block, in a secret room. It was a huge space, big enough to live in. There was even a little kitchen, also mostly hidden behind a dusty plastic tarp. Even if I ignored the construction work, it was hard to feel at home.

Who lived here? Who might come strolling down from the loft?

Kate spun around and said, "Oh, by the way, you should know we have company."

I heard water splashing on the other side of the closed door. Then it opened and a girl I never saw before stepped out. She was tiny, perfectly put together, and her shiny black hair was gathered in a pink bow at the nape of her neck. When she saw me, she looked a little startled.

"How many of us will there be, do you think?" she said. "I am Bet. It's a nickname. It means 'duck' in my country."

She smiled shyly and spoke perfect English, too perfect to have learned the language in the United States.

"Bet is from Thailand," Piper said. "Her family just moved here this year."

Bet and I said hello, and then we had one of those moments where there was so much to say that no one said anything. We dug into the fruit salad, poured lemonade, and finally made some small talk.

"Good cantaloupe," was all I could contribute.

To make conversation, Bet pointed out her locker door. On this side of the world, it had her name written on it, like a movie star's door—Bet Hirujadanpholdoi.

I wanted to turn around and see mine, but the phone on the meeting table rang. Bet let out a squeal and her hands flew up to her face.

"What do we do?" I shrieked, as it rang an old-fashioned-sounding *ring-ring-ring*.

"Pick up," Piper said.

"Pick up, but be polite," Kate added.

I picked up the heavy pink earpiece and said, "Hello?"

"Hello, dear!" a kindly woman's voice called out. "Can you hear me okay? Flick the silver switch on the phone, please."

I snapped the silver toggle to the right, and the woman's voice filled the room. The sound quality was scratchy, like when you're ordering something from a drive-thru. She sounded a little like my Great-Aunt Agnes.

"Let me first say welcome—welcome to you girls. I know this is a little disorienting. Believe me, I know. But this is going to be an important day for all of you!"

She went on to say we four had been selected by "members emeritus" of the Pink Locker Society, formerly the Pink Locker Ladies. This secret organization was dedicated to serving the girls of Margaret Simon Middle School—and had been "since forever," she said.

"Girls, *emeritus* means past, as in golden oldies," she said.

Whoa. We were shocked. A secret society operating in our boring school? I wanted to know more, much more. Like who were last year's society members? They would be in high school now, but at least we could ask them what was up with all of this. But when I asked about last year's group, the woman on the other end of the phone didn't answer.

"Well, there was a . . . an unfortunate interruption in our history. There hasn't been a PLS since the 1970s. Can you hold on a minute?"

Before we could say OK, we heard the woman murmuring to someone else. It seemed like a long time before she got back on the line.

"Well, where were we? You girls have been selected to restart our chapter. This has been years in the making!" she said.

Seeing as we didn't know what she was talking about, we didn't know what to do next. Should we applaud, yell hooray!, or just keep quiet in the hope that she would start making sense? The four of us stayed silent, hoping to hear more.

"Does anyone here know about the PLS?" the woman said.

Kate raised her hand, like she expected to be called on.

"Anyone?" called the voice on the phone, unable to see Kate's raised hand.

I nudged Kate, and she said, "Me."

"That must be Kate," said the voice.

"Kate has been selected for the PLS through one of our most interesting channels. She is what we call a 'legacy'— someone in her family was a Pinky! And now Kate can carry on the noble tradition."

"What the heck does that mean?" Piper asked, her mouth full of grapes.

"Of course, of course you want to know," the woman said. "The PLS serves middle-school girls in need. We have a network of members both current—which means you four—and a number of women throughout the decades. It's a vast network to support you in your work."

Piper looked at me the same way she looked at me earlier today when our English teacher wrote "iambic pentameter" on the board. Kate pursed her lips like she does when she's trying to keep a secret. I gave her a what-gives? sort of look, but she said nothing.

"What is this 'work' of which you speak?" Bet asked in a small voice.

"Sorry, dear. I didn't quite catch that," the voice said.

"I think we—I mean, everyone but Kate—are still a little confused," I told the phone voice.

"Oh, yes, of course!" the woman said. "So little to say, so much time. I mean . . . nevermind . . . reverse that. The Pink Locker Ladies—I mean the Pink Locker Society—performs a valuable service here at Margaret Simon. Any girl who has a problem or question can get it answered quickly, accurately, and with the kindness we have built our history upon!"

Kate stayed quiet, but Piper and I kept asking away.

"What kind of questions?" Piper asked.

"That's what you're going to find out once they start

writing in. In my day, it was a lot about growing into a woman—changing bodies and so forth. Some things change, but I suspect that as long as there are girls, they will want to know about PBBs."

Even Kate was mystified.

"PBBs?"

"Oh, sorry, dear. That's periods, bras, and boys. Nothing draws a crowd of girls better than those topics."

Piper laughed out loud, and Bet's hands flew to her face again. Kate shot me a look and smiled. PBBs were the topics we discussed 99 percent of the time. But none of us, except maybe Piper, would have considered herself an expert.

"How are we going to help them? Take appointments like a doctor?" Piper asked. "I would look really good in a white doctor's coat."

"Oh, no, dear. We give advice confidentially. Back in the day, girls would drop off their questions in little wooden boxes hidden around the school. But today, I'm proud to announce, we're launching PinkLockerSociety.org—an Internet Web site! Isn't technology just marvelous? I e-mail my grandchildren all the time. And have you girls ever seen the YouTube?"

"Yes, we know all about YouTube," I said, smirking a little. "So how will the Web site help girls?"

"Girls will e-mail in their questions, and you'll put the answers up on PinkLockerSociety.org. In fact, we've already been spreading the word in a rather sneaky way. A few of us former Pinkies have slipped pink bookmarks in certain books in the school library. You know, the ones that girls check out most often? The bookmarks tell them about the Web site and this fabulous new service—well, it's actually an old service being delivered in a new way."

"You just went into the school library, and no one noticed? Isn't that trespassing?" Piper asked.

"Well, let's just say we have some former Pinkies on the inside. That's how we managed to get the pink locker doors installed and see that you four didn't get assigned a study hall room. It's great to have Pinkies in high places!"

This was getting more intriguing—the thought of undercover Pinkies walking among us at school.

"Can girls text in their questions?" Piper asked.

"Sure, sure. I think so, anyway. We've hired a technology consultant to get you girls set up. Goodness knows, I wouldn't know where to begin."

"What if we give the wrong advice?" I asked.

"Oh, you won't, dear," she said.

I wasn't convinced. If someone or some book had all the answers about PBBs, I would be happy to learn, I thought. But before we could ask who or where we'd find such a thing, the voice said, "Check your mailboxes on the way out. You already have your first client for the year. I printed out the e-mail for you. Good luck, and think pink!"

28

But I had a question on the tip of my tongue: How could I, someone who knows almost nothing about PBBs, give advice about them? In fact, I could give advice only about one B—bras. And even that was limited to what my mom told me about training bras.

I had a few other questions for the mysterious woman on the other side of the phone: Who was she, this grand-motherly person who never told us her name? How were we going to run a Web site? Why were we picked for this job? Who brought the snacks?

When the speakerphone fell silent, Bet was the first to speak.

"Are we getting graded on this?"

Piper and Kate both laughed, but I didn't know if Bet was serious or making a joke. And who was Bet anyway? I wondered if she would be hanging out with us now. Me, Kate, and Piper were the Gleeful Threeful, as my mom always called us. It had been that way ever since we were toddlers. Our moms met at Yoga Baby class and we'd been entwined like pretzels ever since.

"I am so totally jazzed about this," Piper said, spinning around in a high-backed chair at the conference table. "I feel like a business tycoon in here!"

"What are we supposed to do now?" I asked.

Before Kate could answer, we heard the bell ring. It was 2:10, the end of study hall. Instantly, pink lanterns I hadn't noticed before switched on. They were posted above our locker doors, like torches to light our way. It lit up the doorways so we could see our mailboxes too.

Our individual doors—with our names on them—were in three of the four walls. I originally thought we formed a triangle, like a mysterious pyramid. But Bet's door and my door shared the same wall. At best, the four of us formed same kind of trapezoid.

"Call me tonight!" Kate called as we split up to go back through our lockers. Before I opened the pink door, I grabbed a thick stack of papers from my mailbox—a plastic pocket at my locker door. It was sort of like the mailboxes I'd seen in the teachers' lounge. Then I took a big step up, carefully clearing the step I fell down on the way in.

The inside of my locker was dark. And I wondered how I would pop out of it unnoticed. I waited for the sounds of people walking past to fade away, slowly pulled up on the inside latch, and stepped back into the real world as the light spilled in.

Eight

On the bus ride home, I sat alone and started reading my PLS mail. I devoured it, looking for more information that would make this picture come into focus. Even though I knew more than I did on the first day of school, it was still pretty fuzzy. There was some helpful stuff in my stack of mail, including a short history of the PLS.

There was a calendar that included our regular meetings (every school day during study hall) and the word combination for each day. Next up was R-E-S-P-E-C-T. The packet also included an entire pad of hall passes in case our work took us out of the office during study hall. (Cool!) And there was a key labeled "elevator." (?!) Then I came to the e-mail printout about our first assignment. It said our first client was a sixth-grade girl, identified only as MG, who submitted the following question:

Dear PLS,

I'm in sixth grade, and my best friend already has her period. I want mine but also sort of don't. I need to know **exactly** *when it will come. It needs to come soon and not at school for the first time. Please help! I don't know what to do, and I can't talk to my mom. Too embarrassing!*

Your friend,
MG

The question hit me like an ice cream headache. Just when I was starting to think I might like this Pink Locker Society stuff, POW! Here I was, an eighth-grader, and not only did I not have the answers to MG's question, I was still waiting for *my* period. I couldn't imagine sitting around that big conference table in the PLS office, admitting to Piper and Bet that I didn't have my period and dreaming up some answer for the 6GG.

I was pretty sure I was the only eighth-grader who had this problem, but only Kate knew I was still waiting. Piper always assumed that I had mine. She even once asked me for a pad because she forgot hers at home. Luckily, I always keep them with me, just in case. But before I could get too deep into MG's question or think much about my situation, I read an instruction in bold type on the title page of the file:

STOP. Do NOT answer any client's question until you have read the PLS Rule Book.

I leafed through my thick bundle of mail and fished out a slim gray book. It looked used, like something you'd find in your grandma's attic. But finally, here were the rules. They began on the first inside page.

Failure to read and follow each of these rules will result in immediate dismissal!

At this point, I wasn't sure I even wanted to be in the Pink Locker Society, and this was telling me how easy it would be to get kicked out. Still, the handbook was a happy discovery. Here's what the handbook said on page four:

1. Enter the PLS office only during study hall—five minutes after the final bell.
2. Give high-quality advice. Don't guess. Learn and share your knowledge.
3. The PLS is a secret organization. Do not talk about your work or give the pink locker combination to **anyone** under **any** circumstances.
4. The PLS is not a clique. To honor our history of grace and kindness, be a friend to all.
5. If you get in a jam, issue a PLS-SOS.

I understood some of the rules completely, but others left me completely clueless. What on earth was a PLS-SOS? If it meant a desperate plea for help, I was ready to ask for one right now—even before the school bus I was riding on stopped at my street. At that moment, the bus did stop. We were at the entrance to Forrest's neighborhood. I looked up to lovingly follow the back of his head down the aisle and down the bus stairs. It was then that he *turned around* in his seat, found me *three rows back*, and said, "Hey" before turning to leave. This particular *hey* from Forrest, combined with the extra effort involved in turning around, was practically an aloha.

Unfortunately, I didn't have a quick or witty response. He just caught me so off guard. I guess my eyes were focused on the front of the bus, watching him leave, so I called out, "Watch your step!" That's right. Instead of saying something cool or funny, I yelled out what it says on that big sign right next to the bus driver. I immediately ducked my head and wished I could hide completely, like a turtle in its shell.

Nine

You might guess I spent all that loooooong weekend thinking about the PLS and talking about it with my friends. But you would be wrong. I spent most of the weekend thinking about what (actually, who) I usually think about most—Forrest Charles McCann. Here's the deal: Forrest is not my boyfriend. He never was my boyfriend, and he shows no signs of wanting to be my boyfriend. In fact, one big sign that he does not want to be my boyfriend is his very real girlfriend, Taylor Mayweather.

Yes, *that* Taylor.

The one who embarrasses people as, like, her hobby. Still, my crush on Forrest runs deep and feels important. These feelings started small way back when Forrest's family and my family used to vacation together. My heart always tells me this will go somewhere, even if it's taking the long way. I liked dwelling on the rumor that Taylor was completely flirting with this guy Gabe, who was nice and geeky-smart. Some people said she was two-timing Forrest. I could only hope it was true and that he would eventually break up with her.

Kate doubted this would happen. She also was not as impressed with Forrest's *hey* to me on the bus.

"You fall into a mysterious office in our school, then find out you're part of a secret society," she said. "And you still want to talk about what Forrest might have meant when he said hey?"

Easy for Kate to say. She's had the same boyfriend (princely Paul) since fifth grade. Not so for me. And anyway, this was a hey worth analyzing. It seemed logical to me that the PLS—remarkable as it was—couldn't push Forrest from my daydreams. No matter what I was thinking about, most roads led back to Forrest. I could bring almost any subject back to him.

Example: A toothpaste commercial with a hot guy in it. The Forrest Connection? He once told me he brushes his teeth with warm water. Weird!

Example: Someone says our football team is supposed to be really good this year. The Forrest Connection? Easy! Forrest is *on* the football team.

Example: Mom says we're going to Cedar Park Shopping Plaza. The FC? We will be driving *right by* Forrest's house. Hopefully, he'll be out front mowing the lawn.

Example: I've just been selected by a secret society that meets behind pink locker doors. The FC? What if he sees me climbing inside? Or, on the bright side, maybe I could sneak him into the PLS office, just for a quick peek.

That last one is sooooo tempting, because when you are in love with an eighth-grade boy, you really need to come up with things to talk about. Maybe you already know that eighth-grade boys really don't talk that much. Oh, sure, you hear them laughing and talking with their friends or sometimes with their coaches. But just put one of them alone with one girl (especially a nervous one who likes him). If, on top of your nerves, you don't have a single thing to talk about, the silence will bruise your heart and leave you with nothing—absolutely nothing—to analyze later.

I heard that kind of silence the last time Forrest and I were alone together. We were on the seventh-grade ski trip and accidentally ended up sharing the same chairlift. The pairing was a shock, but I tried to recover quickly and take advantage of our time together. It went about as well as the "Watch your step!" catastrophe on the bus.

Why is it OK for girls and boys to be friends until third grade, and then everything gets totally weird? That was the year when people started saying that Forrest and I were boyfriend and girlfriend, which we were not. Not really. We were just friends who could play knock out on the basketball court at recess, or we'd sometimes play desktop football with one of those folded-up triangles of notebook paper. Maybe he got tired of answering the boyfriend-girlfriend rumors, because he stopped hanging around me and started hanging out only with the boys. Even when he came to our house, he'd hang out with the grown-ups or with his younger brother. And then came Taylor.

So it had been *years* since we'd really talked when the ski lift brought us together. It was a long ride up a steep mountain on a cold, sun-splashed morning. I started slowly, asking him how he was.

"Okay," he said.

"I love to ski, don't you?"

"It's cool," he said.

"Your skis are really nice."

"They're rentals," he said.

"My mom wanted me to wear a helmet today, but I said no."

"You should," he said, knocking the hard plastic of the helmet on his own head.

"Yeah, but I didn't want it to squish my hair, because then it gets all flat and stuff."

To that, Forrest had nothing to say. What could he say, really? What does a guy know about helmet hair? We spent the rest of the ride in silence, as I searched the landscape desperately for something to talk about. But there was nothing to say about the tops of trees or the few clouds in the sky. We climbed higher and I could feel the temperature fall. The soft snow cushioned what little sound there was from other skiers and snowboarders below. My ears popped. Then the lift stopped, as it sometimes does when a little kid can't get on or someone drops a pole. We bobbed together on the thick cable. The quiet hung there with us, and I was sure that I was blowing my one chance with Forrest. I thought about what Kate and Piper would do in the same situation.

Kate was good at telling stories, and she would have reminded Forrest of something funny that happened when we were younger. There were tons of possibilities. The Halloween in kindergarten when our moms made us dress as a bride and groom. The time we had a wiener roast while camping and ate hotdogs that were charred black on the outside and icy in the center. (We called them "hotdogsicles.") I actually had plenty of material, plenty of *topics*. There were field trips and mean teachers and so many other things we had seen together over the years. But not a single one of them came to mind on that ski lift.

As for Piper, well, you know what she would have done in my place. She would have told him that she liked him, flat out. And then she would have looked at him through her long eyelashes. He would have melted, as most guys do when Piper flirts with them. But me, I couldn't even glance in his direction, let alone attempt that chin-down, gaze-up, bat eyelashes thing Piper does. I refocused my energies on what I'd say when we hopped off the lift at the top. I sooooooo wanted to say something like "Have a great run" or "See you at the bottom." But I ended up saying nothing. Why? Because at the top of the hill, someone stopped me dead in my tracks. She was waiting for Forrest, her fur-trimmed hood the perfect frame for her face flushed pink with cold. It was Taylor Mayweather.

Ten

Our plan for Monday was this: We would have our own pre-meeting, without Bet, at lunch, giving us time to collect our thoughts before our real meeting at 1:35. The girls had given me tips and even had me practice the pink locker combination that morning. At lunch, I sat down with my pizza and milk and was ready to talk about the PLS. Here's what I wanted to go over:

- None of us has an assigned room for study hall. Discuss the potential negatives, such as getting caught and having less time to do homework.
- What happens if we are in the secret office during a fire drill?
- Ask the group: Can I show someone (like, say, Forrest

McCann) the PLS office as long as I don't give out the combination or "discuss our work," as prohibited in rule three?

But Kate and Piper wanted to get right to work on MG's question.

Great, but don't ask me. No-period girl has zero advice to give about periods.

I tried to stay very quiet and took tiny bites of my pizza so I could be chewing every time there was a break in the conversation.

"I got mine in sixth, so I think we should tell her to start worrying if she doesn't get hers by the end of the year," Piper said, spearing a forkful of her Caesar salad.

"I don't know. I don't think we should be telling her to worry," Kate said. "We should just tell her to hang in there. You can't schedule it like a dentist appointment. Periods happen when they happen."

Kate looked at me knowingly.

"Yeah, but shouldn't she go to the doctor if it, like, never comes? Maybe there's something wrong with her," Piper said.

They went back and forth for a while and couldn't decide what to say to MG. When they turned to me, I pointed to my chewing mouth and shrugged. But as the conversation went on, I started to feel a little better. The truth was, here were two girls who had their periods, and even they didn't know what to tell MG. So my not knowing was beginning to seem like less of a big deal. Of course, this was also a problem, because if we couldn't give MG a good answer, maybe we wouldn't cut it as the new members of the Pink Locker Society.

When the girls turned to me for, like, the forty-fourth time, I had just swallowed the last square inch of my pizza. Kate's eyes widened as they turned to me, knowing how I didn't want to talk about this one. But luckily, the rules were there to bail me out.

"Well, rule number two says: 'Give high-quality advice. Don't guess. Learn and share your knowledge.' We better do some research at the library or something."

"Where did it say that?" Piper asked.

"In the handbook, page four."

I held my breath, but they both agreed.

"Ugh, the library," Piper said.

"I love the library," Kate said. "We can go tonight."

"Me too," I said.

We stood up and, as I did, I took note of where Forrest was in the cafeteria—sitting with the other football players and Taylor, as usual. I would have to pass right by them on my way to take back my tray. I allowed myself a quick glance—long enough to notice that Taylor was not only sitting at his table, she was sharing his chair!

As if she knew I was watching, Taylor threw back her head and laughed like Forrest had said the funniest thing she'd ever heard. I tried to look away but just couldn't. Then, for a flash, Forrest saw me. He didn't smile, but he didn't *not* smile, either. His in-between expression was even harder to figure out than the *hey* from the bus. *Watch your step, Taylor,* I thought. Yeah, right. You know who should watch her step? Me.

Eleven

*L*ater that day, at study hall time, I confidently opened my locker and waited until everyone else had drifted away. When I was alone, I thrust my hand in to open the pink locker and grabbed the combination dial. I was prepared for the lighting issues this time with my key chain that has a little green flashlight on the end. With one hand, I sent a bolt of green light toward the combination dial. With my other hand, I spelled out R-E-S-P-E-C-T. I was in. I even closed the door quietly and stepped *ever so carefully* down the too-tall step and placed both feet securely on the thick rose rug.

In fact, I was the first girl in the office and was able to look around without any distractions for about thirty seconds. What I saw made me feel once again like I was dreaming.

The old-lady furnishings and the dusty tarps were gone. It was spotlessly clean and completely renovated. It looked like a ritzy hotel suite. The place could have been on TV or in the movies, like if someone was running a modeling agency.

On one side of the room, there was now a U-shaped pink couch with a glass table in the center. Floral arrangements had been added to the now-dust-free conference table. The old pink phone had been replaced by a sleek black model. Silver appliances gleamed from the kitchen. Lifting my head toward the loft (aided this time by my glasses), I could see a row of computers giving off a green glow.

The only trace of the old office was a pile of machines at the foot of the stairs. Turns out they weren't sewing machines after all. They were typewriters: super-old black ones with no power cords and newer (but still old) electric ones that were aqua and must have weighed fifty pounds each.

Kate was next to arrive, and she just stood in one spot, taking in all the changes. Piper arrived next. "No way!" she said of the sparkling new faucets, stone countertops, and monogrammed hand towels. Not PLS, as you might expect, but P, J, K, and B—one for each of us.

"Who is paying for this?" Piper wanted to know.

"The Pinkies, apparently," Kate said as she picked up a note that had been left next to the snacks on the table.

We watched her scan the note. As she held it up, I could

see through the back side of the rose-colored stationery. The writer had the formal, forward-leaning handwriting of a teacher or grandmother.

"It says that we're the new generation of the Pink Locker Society, and they wanted to give us a 'well-appointed, comfortable place to work,'" Kate said.

"May I?" Piper said, pinching a corner of the note and taking it.

"Hmmm . . . 'For reasons you can understand, those who have endowed the new PLS shall remain anonymous.' And it's signed 'Edith.'"

"She must be the one who called us the first day," I said, "She never gave her name."

"So the retired Pinkies have some dough. That's good news," Piper said.

"Hey, where's Bet?" Kate asked. "She's missing all the fun."

Long after the golden minute had passed, Bet was still nowhere to be found. We went to her locker and opened it from the office side. It was dark.

"Should we, like, look for her or something?" Piper asked.

"Did anyone see her today?" Kate asked.

I hadn't, but I also hadn't really looked. The truth is I would have liked it better if it was just the three of us. Having a fourth person, who was a complete stranger, made everything more confusing. Like at lunch today, we decided to go to the library, and now we'd have to bring her up to speed and invite her along, etc.

Before we could even begin to really search for Bet, the conference-table phone rang. I picked it up and clicked the red button so everyone could hear. It was a new voice coming in crystal clear over the new phone. This one was a younger woman with a Minnesota accent. That's where my dad's from.

"Hiya, girls," she said. "Things are lookin' pretty good there, eh?"

We murmured our agreement.

"Okey-doke. Is everybody ready to do a little high-tech work today?" she asked.

"Uh, sure?" I said, a little wary.

"Ah, that's great! Why don't ya move upstairs where the computers are and put me on the phone up there?"

"Will do," I said.

Up in the loft, we turned on the speakerphone, and there she was again.

"Pretty nice setup, wouldn't ya say?" she asked from the speaker box. "Ya got the Infinitrix 3,000 system up here, the same computers they use in the White House."

It was awfully nice in the loft. The computer desks were whitewashed wood, and the chairs were those fancy super-comfortable ones that they sell in the back of magazines for eight hundred dollars. "Whose behind is worth eight hundred dollars?" my mother would say when she saw those ads. But you just felt important sitting down in a chair like that. The PLS computers started up quickly—nothing like the chugging old computer we had in our basement family room.

After we all sat down and logged in, the woman on the phone told us that she was going to give us a "lickety-split" lesson in how to run the Pink Locker Society Web site. All we needed to do was learn a few basics and we'd be able to do it on our own. In other words, we soon could post MG's answer. If we had an answer for her.

But before our computer lesson could get going, the woman on the phone stopped and asked us where Bet was. We had all created usernames and passwords for our new computers.

"I don't see her signed in here," she said.

"She didn't show," Piper said. "We opened her pink locker, but she wasn't there."

"Aw, that's a darn shame. This is a pretty important session," she said. "You'll hafta fill her in later."

It was right then that Kate and I had one of those friend-ESP moments. We both had exactly the same thought at exactly the same time: Bet's pink locker door was still open. If Bet did happen to show up late, she would open her regular locker and give the whole world an inside look at our secret world!

Before I moved a muscle, Kate leaped down the stairs of the loft. *Slam!* Mission accomplished, Kate returned to her desk in time to get a tour of the Pink Locker Society Web site. It had way-cool music and one of those fancy intros. Then the bright pink page opened up, but it said only "Coming soon! Very soon!" Nothing like a little pressure.

The woman on the phone told us it would be "just great" if we could get our first answer up there by "Wednesday or thereabouts." That was two days away.

"Ya don't want to leave gals in the lurch, ya know," she said.

Piper mouthed, "We are dead."

Kate waved Piper off and asked the woman another question about what it meant for something to be "live" on the Web site. She explained that "live" meant something had been published on the Web site. It was there for everyone to see. No one would be able to benefit from our advice if we didn't get something live, she said.

In twenty minutes, she had me thinking that it wasn't as hard as I thought to run a Web site. The site—www. PinkLockerSociety.org—was already designed for us. It was like a set of blank pages that we needed to fill. We created test questions and answers and watched them instantly fill the front page of PinkLockerSociety.org.

Kate asked: Q. How much wood can a woodchuck chuck?

And I answered: A. As much as Forrest McCann tells him to.

And *voila!* It was on the front page of the PLS Web site.

We quickly deleted it so no one would think we'd lost our minds.

Piper flew right through our tutorial and asked all kinds of questions about the firewall and whether our servers had received the recent JDK upgrade. She's scary smart with technical stuff, and she also types way faster than any of us. So it was easy to decide who should be the primary owner of the sweet pink laptop we were allowed to take with us into the outside world. Piper said she'd fix it so that questions submitted to the PLS would come right to our phones.

"Best of luck to ya, girls," our computer consultant said. "And Piper, call me if ya have any more questions about what's going on under the hood!"

With that, our training was over. It was up to us to start a Web site and continue the Pink Locker Society legacy. I still had so many questions. It would have made me feel better to talk, in person, to some former PLS members. Who was it that Kate knew in the old PLS? Maybe she could tell us what happened all those years ago to shut down the PLS? But most of all, I wanted to know: Why restart now, and why us?

But in the pink crush of everything, I didn't say a word. Study hall would be over soon so I hustled to my locker door and checked my mailbox. Edith had printed out the new questions that had come in since Friday. I paused to scan them. I guess I shouldn't have been surprised, but two of them were similar questions about periods, including one from another eighth-grader. So I wasn't the only one! Weird body changes, boys, problems with friends, too much homework—these subjects came up a lot.

There was even one in there from a girl with really big boobs! She wrote:

> *This is going to sound weird, but my boobs are ruining my life. They are ENOR-MOOSE boobs. Biggest in the whole school.*

I really had to hurry now. I stood only a moment in the dark of my locker, eager to get back into the light and read the rest of her question. I would give anything to have an ENOR-MOOSE boob problem. I should have stopped longer to listen for people in the hall. If I had, I might not have walked right into Taylor and Clementine's big fight.

Twelve

aylor's ever-present sidekick, Tia, was holding the big TV light and working the video camera, as she always did for the MSTV broadcasts. Taylor was this year's anchor for Margaret Simon TV, our in-school channel that was beamed into all the classrooms once a week, whether you liked it or not. Last year, Clem was the anchor, and it seemed she was not ready to give up her spot. She had mostly used the privilege to film *Clem's Crib*, a reality show starring . . . guess who.

"There's no rule against someone being anchor two years in a row," Clem told Taylor, getting right in her face. "We should have an *experienced* reporter, not just someone who does stories about kittens."

"That was just my audition tape. People love kittens, so I knew I'd get the job," Taylor said.

Do you see why I can't stand her?

"And besides, my real show isn't about kittens. It's much edgier than that," she said.

"Yeah, right. You're about as edgy as a kitten, Taylor. But you are sneaky. What a coincidence that I was out of town when you guys had your supposed meeting," Clem said.

"Not my problem," Taylor said, flipping open a gold compact to check her lip gloss.

MSTV was organized as a student club and overseen by our art teacher, Ms. Russo. She also does the school plays, teaches interpretive dance, and once brought in a live sheep for us to sketch. She's a little kooky and lets the kids run the show, literally.

Clem (being Clem) probably expected to get the anchor job again, no questions asked. No one looks better on camera, that's true. But the gossip around school was that Taylor grabbed control at a summertime meeting for kids interested in the TV club. Clem was in Bali on a photo shoot, apparently. With Tia on Taylor's side (Tia knows how to work the camera and edit the video), what else did she need?

When I popped out of my locker, I'd like to say Taylor and Clem were so locked in battle that neither one noticed me. No such luck. Clem did look rattled, though. Her face—usually a porcelain pale—looked pink and angry. But it was Taylor who saw me first, lowering her compact to get a better look. When my two feet hit the floor, I looked up, and she was looking right at me. Tia's video-camera light illuminated Taylor so that, from where I was, her white-blond hair glowed like an angel. Tia cut the light, and Clem spun around to see me, too.

"What were you doing in your locker?" Taylor snapped.

"I was just . . . getting stuff," I stammered.

"With the door closed?" Taylor asked.

"I'm late," I said, breaking into one of those awkward speed walks. I acted like I had somewhere to be, but the first bell hadn't even rung yet.

"There's your next *big* story, Taylor," Clem said, tossing her head in that top-model way, "—people who hide in their lockers. Film at eleven." Then Clem flicked her stick-straight hair over her shoulder and left Taylor and Tia alone in the hall with the video camera running.

Thirteen

et was waiting for us outside at the end of the day, as the buses stacked up against the curb. I knew she was short, but she looked even smaller next to the buses. Her long black hair was swept back in a red headband. She wore skinny black jeans and a red denim jacket. Around her ankle she wore a tiny gold anklet with a red stone, probably a real ruby, that dipped down over her delicate anklebone. Her face looked pained, like it might crack, and she held her head as if there were a book balanced on top of it.

"How was the meeting? Please, excuse me for not being there. Sincere apologies."

"Where were you?" Piper asked sharply.

"I . . . I had something I needed to do, " Bet stuttered.

"You missed computer training, but we can show how it all works," Kate said.

"Um, okay, well, I'm not sure I'd be very good with computer stuff anyway. Maybe I could just do office tasks. Stuff envelopes or answer the phone?"

"The phone might ring once a day, and no one stuffs anything," Piper said. "Well, Jemma stuffs her bra, but I don't think she needs help."

Piper hugged me around the shoulders to show she was kidding.

"Aren't you just hysterical," I said in a monotone.

"Bet, maybe you don't want to be part of the PLS," I said, watching for her reaction as my words hit the air.

Bet's brown eyes looked into mine. She looked hurt. You would have thought someone had just accused *her* of bra stuffing.

"Jem, don't push her out the door," Kate said.

Kate seemed fine about not including Bet in our lunch meeting, but now good-deed Kate was in the house.

"I'm not pushing her out the door," I said. "I'm just saying the PLS is optional."

Knowing I already hurt Bet's feelings, I continued, trying to soften my position.

"I mean, it is a lot of work, and it *will* leave less time for studying."

This time, Bet kept her eyes squarely on a crack in the sidewalk at her feet. The truth was, I would have liked to push her out. But Kate, being Kate, insisted.

"Bet, we're meeting at the college library at six thirty to do some research. Meet us there and we'll fill you in."

As I walked to my bus, my worries quickly switched from Bet to Forrest. What if Taylor had already told him what she saw? I could just imagine her saying, "Oh my gosh, you should've seen Jemma today, she's so weird. She was hiding inside her locker!"

Fourteen

Bet didn't show at the library, and I could tell Kate blamed me. Kate almost always does the right thing. If you have a friend like Kate, you know how that is. I love her for being honest and kind, but sometimes I feel like I can't compare.

Could I have been more welcoming to Bet? Sure. But I didn't like that our trio of friends had suddenly become a quartet.

At the library, it looked for a minute like Piper wouldn't come either, but she finally arrived and we picked a study carrel away from all the people working so quietly. We searched the library—and online—for information about periods. It turns out that periods are pretty complicated. In books, people call them a hundred different things: menstruation, menarche, menses. (I've heard it called "Aunt Flo" and "the curse," which it definitely is not, because if it were, why would I want it so bad?) The books' explanations for what actually goes on inside the body were so technical ("the shedding of the endometrium," blah, blah, blah) and did not help us answer MG's question at all. But finally, after searching a bunch of books and Web sites, we had some information for her—and me.

Piper, Kate, and I were feeling good now that we had an answer for our first client. I couldn't tell if I was just relieved over the comforting information we'd found about periods or if I was happy to be able to help someone. It was nice to think of MG out there feeling better after she read our answer.

"This could be fun, I think," I whispered across the table.

"Yes, but what do we tell the girl with the enor-MOOSE boobs?" Kate whispered back.

"That's easy. I know all about that," Piper said, pushing her chest in our direction. Then, in dramatic fashion, she shared her three tips for girls blessed with big bazooms:

1. Do the cleavage check. Stand in front of a mirror and bend over. If you can see down your shirt, don't wear it.
2. Wear a supportive bra that's the right size.

3. If someone looks too long at your chest, say, "Yo, my eyes are up here."

I was excited that we now had two answers ready for the Pink Locker Web site. We still had a little time before my mom picked us up, so Kate headed over to the archives and told Piper and me to take up the third client question about whether or not to tell your crush you like him.

We couldn't find a single book in the library that gave advice about the tell-or-not-tell issue. But Piper and I agreed that people have been asking this question for a long time. Even really old stories, like the ones my mom sometimes reads to me out loud, seemed to be about love. Piper reminded me that this plot had been well explored by several TV shows. I was not at all sure whether it was better to love someone secretly or to reveal that love and very possibly get your heart squished.

I also wasn't sure that Piper would be much help on the subject. Sure, she knew what it was like to be crushed on, since so many boys liked her. But I didn't think she had a Forrest McCann on her mind all the time. It was as if she read my mind with what she said next:

"You know, everyone has a Forrest McCann."

For a minute, I was worried that she was going to tell me she also liked Forrest, which would pretty much eliminate me from having any chance with him. But then she continued.

"I like someone right now and I don't know whether to tell him," Piper said. "On the one hand, you want to know if he likes you, too. But what if he doesn't?"

Whoa. We shared more common ground than I thought. Who was her Forrest McCann? And what about Jamie Welch, who was supposedly her boyfriend right now?

Finally, she gave up the name.

"It's Jonah Zafron," Piper said.

"You're thinking of telling the *movie star* Jonah Zafron that you have a crush on him?"

"Don't you think he would want to know?" she said, giving me that flirty look she used so well on cute boys.

Before I could remind her how old Jonah was or that he already had a girlfriend, Kate returned from the archives with a stack of papers. She slapped them down in front of us, and together we read the headline of *The Pink Paper*, published in October 1976. In big, blaring type, it said: PINK LOCKER SOCIETY IN DANGER! But the headline was all we could read. Every line of the article had been blacked out.

Fifteen

If you were to visit www.PinkLockerSociety.org, here's what you'd see today. Ta-dah! Our first answers for our first clients:

To MG, the girl who was worried about not getting her period:

Dear MG,

You can breathe a sigh of relief: Plenty of girls do NOT have their periods by sixth grade. The first period happens during puberty, which can start between ages eight and thirteen. But the key word is START. Some girls start at eight and some start at thirteen. After it gets going, puberty takes a while and lasts for a few years. Most girls get their periods between the ages of ten and fifteen. Everyone is different, but your period usually happens about two years after your breasts start developing.

Unfortunately, periods don't come by appointment. You won't know until it arrives. If your first period (aka "Aunt Flo") arrives for the first time when you're at school, don't panic. Instead, be prepared by keeping a couple of pads in your backpack or locker. If you need help, ask a friend or a female teacher. If you stain your clothes (this hardly ever happens, because first periods are usually light), wrap a sweater or sweatshirt around your waist until you can change.

And we understand how you feel about your period. It's OK to want it and it's OK to not want it, even at the same time! Anything new is weird for a while. It's also more than OK to talk about your feelings with your mom or another girl or woman you are close to. If you need some questions answered, why not ask someone who knows Aunt Flo quite well!

Think pink!
The PLS

I keep track of all my major successes in life. The list is not that long, but I'm happy to say that I think today is one of them. We answered not only MG's period question but also the one about big boobs and the one about crushes.

We used Piper's advice about getting your chest stared at. Thank you, Piper!

And what about the crush question?

After a lot of thought—and a conversation with Kate's older sister—we offered this advice to the person who wrote that they kinda-sorta wanted to tell their crush about their true feelings.

Dear DM,

People have been asking your question for hundreds of years, and the answer is not crystal clear. Crushes are called crushes for a reason. They can hit you hard! And it can feel amazing to learn that your crush likes you, too. Imagine Christmas morning and your birthday combined. Woo-hoo! But when the person doesn't have a crush on you, it can feel like a dozen rainy Mondays all at once.

The good news is that crushes are like playing make-believe. It's probably been a long time since you did that! But crushes are a way of imagining, thinking about, and even testing out what it is like to fall in love. So it's up to you if you want to take a risk and see if your crush likes you, too. Are you feeling brave? Or maybe you'll decide that your crush is more fun kept as a secret. The only thing we know for sure is that this won't be your last crush.

Happy crushing!
The PLS

We felt really good to post those answers. But we felt even better when we went to the PLS office, signed on to our computers, and saw that the Web site had gotten more than one hundred visitors by lunchtime! I even heard some girls talking about it in the bathroom. Not only that, but lots of people sent us e-mail *thanking* us. Here are a few:

OMG, you guys soooooo rock. I was very worried about "Aunt Flo," and now I know exactly what to do when she makes her first visit. Thank you! Thank you!
Signed,
A not-so-nervous-anymore seventh-grader

I have had a crush on someone for a long time and now I feel mucho bettero.
Your friend—BBallGRL98

Thank you, PLS! I am feeling less worried and much more un-shy now about periods. I think I might ask my mom about it. After all, she was young once. I've seen pictures!
Keep up the good work,
MG

DM, the crush girl, and the girl with the big boobs hadn't written back yet, but I hoped they liked our answers. Walking around school, I felt different. I couldn't put my finger on it, but I guessed this confident feeling must be what it feels like to be popular. I was sort of a celebrity, even though no one knew who I was.

Sixteen

person can get used to almost anything, my mother often says. She's even written a poem about it—one of the many I don't completely understand. On one hand, it's great that people can adapt and get used to new stuff. Kate, Piper, and I quickly got used to the fact that we were part of a secret society. In the same way that I trundle off to the caf for lunch at 11:47, I now go to my locker every day at 1:35 and crawl inside (and try not to get caught on the way out).

Beforehand, I write that day's pink locker combination in the palm of my left hand. No one ever asks why I've inked myself with words like B-L-O-O-M, L-E-A-D-E-R, and T-R-U-T-H.

In our headquarters, I grab the daily snack (the fudgy

no-bake cookies are my favorite) and we take care of business. As predicted, PBBs account for most of our inquiries. But there have been other questions on the fringes. One girl asked about what to do if you're afraid to get your ears pierced. And we've even had a couple questions from boys. They mostly want to know about girls and what to do if you like someone—so similar to the kind of questions girls ask!

We're getting so much "business" now that we're working during every study hall and tapping away on the pink laptop during evenings and weekends. (Great, but not so great for my grades.) As promised, Piper rigged our laptop to buzz our phones with a special ringtone when we have a new question. For the ringtone, she recorded the three of us saying "Think pink!"

I feel overwhelmed sometimes, but I still squeeze the PLS into my life, just like I squeeze in track practice (now that I've gotten used to running those endless laps and hilly trails). And also like track, being in the Pink Locker Society makes me feel good, as if I'm an important part of something. I love it when I hear people buzzing about the Web site or wondering who runs the Pink Locker Society. I've even seen "The Pink Locker Society Rocks!" written on the inside of one of the girls' bathroom stalls. And I did eventually find a school library book that had one of those Pink Locker Society bookmarks inside. It said: "They're cool and confidential. Ask and the Pink Locker Society will answer!"

That's me: I'm cool and confidential. It's like an awesome secret, and even though I have had trouble keeping secrets before, I don't mind keeping this one. But this secret would be more fun to keep if it were just between me, Piper, and Kate. If you ask me, Bet is a half-time, half-hearted member. (Which takes its toll on the rest of us, as if she doesn't realize.) She misses a lot of meetings and has answered only a handful of questions from our readers. She barely says anything, just nods a lot and hangs close to Kate.

Plus, Bet hasn't really spoken to me since that day by the buses. I guess she has gotten used to being the new girl, so quiet you hardly know she's there, always hanging on the outskirts. Even though I see her almost every day, I have to admit I have gotten used to something, too—not being Bet's friend.

Seventeen

Friday was always my favorite day of the week, but not anymore. Now we're forced to watch Margaret Simon TV during last period. It was one thing watching Clem parade around during *Clem's Crib*, saying things like "Here's my shoe closet; here's my at-home foot spa for pedicures. . . ." It was sometimes dull, but not the worst way to waste ten minutes of class time. But now that Taylor's the anchor, everything has changed. Of course, since she's Forrest's girlfriend, I didn't exactly long to watch her on TV. But my mood went from bored to electrified today when Forrest called my name on the way into class. I heard him say, "Jemma," but by the time I turned around in my seat, Mr. Ford said, "Face front; let's be courteous during Taylor's broadcast." When I looked back again at Forrest, he just laid his head on his folded arms, like he was going to take a nap.

To prove something to Clem (or maybe all of us), Taylor had dramatically changed her approach to her broadcast. The kittens were definitely gone. Music boomed loudly in the intro to a new show she called *Gotcha!* It began with a scene from a recent football game, with the cheerleaders all posed in a perfect pyramid. Perfect at least until Marina Testarosa wobbled from her perch at the very top and they all came tumbling down. The class laughed a little, and the camera turned again to Taylor, who smiled in a pink turtleneck and said, "Gotcha!"

From there the report went to a tape of Clem Caritas standing in front of the girls' bathroom mirror, putting on lipstick and trying different smiles—the first one big and movie-star-like and the next one shy and closed lipped. Then she winked at herself. "Gotcha!" purred Taylor again, this time pointing a jaunty finger at the camera.

And so it went on for ten uncomfortable minutes, showing people caught on secret videotape. Even though he said nothing, I could tell Mr. Ford was getting annoyed by the way he sighed and shifted in his squeaky desk chair.

"It's funny, right? I think it's really funny," Taylor explained, live to the class.

That seemed to give them more permission to laugh, and they did so with increasing volume with each new clip. The one of Mr. Updike, the janitor, chasing a groundhog around the front lawn drew a real hoot. Hardly anyone laughed, though, when the camera zoomed into the cafeteria, zeroing in on a long lunch table where Bet sat alone, eating delicately from her lunchbox.

"Boo-hoo-hoo and . . . Gotcha!" Taylor said, rubbing her eyes and putting on a fake sad pout.

Just as I was gathering some sympathy for Bet and despising Taylor that much more, I saw a familiar row of lockers emerge on the screen. Then the camera moved in close to catch me slipping out of my locker and stepping a foot gingerly on the linoleum tiles. My face couldn't hide my surprise and, with cheeks flushed pink, I hustled by the camera until Tia could do nothing else but record my fast departure down the hall.

Back to Taylor, who this time said, "Gotcha, Locker Girl!" and narrowed her eyes into a "Could she be any weirder?" kind of look.

My mom often says that we don't absorb difficult things all at once, but rather in stages. My first stage here was breathless shock. I would have gotten up to leave the room, but I was paralyzed in place. Everyone looked at me, some of them still laughing. I could not bring myself to turn around and look at Forrest. My worst fear had come true.

The second stage for me was an incredible desire to just do something—anything. Running away wasn't my first choice, once I had a moment to think. What I wanted to do most was lift Taylor—desk and all—and fling her like a whirlybird out the classroom's second-floor window.

The third stage was trying to make sense of it all. Of course (my brain finally reasoned), Tia had the camera rolling that day in the hallway when I caught Taylor and Clem fighting. And what it captured was not just the cat-fight between them but my odd reentry into the hallway. I was now officially the weirdest girl in school, worse than Bet eating alone or Clem smiling at herself in the bathroom. I was someone who spent time inside her locker with the door closed.

Thankfully, Taylor's segment soon ended, and Mr. Ford grumbled something about moving along because the buses were already lining up. I started to gather myself but I felt like I was moving in slow motion, having to think about each step I took: *Pick up backpack, step with the right foot, now with the left.* Kate and Piper ran up to me after class, but I couldn't even talk.

"What a beast, she is—like that Jerry Springsteen on TV," Piper said.

"It's Jerry Springer. Springsteen is the singer," Kate corrected. "Are you okay?" she asked me.

"No," I said meekly. I walked with great effort to my bus, like I was walking through deep, deep snow.

To my surprise, someone was standing at the bus's door, waiting for me. It was Forrest.

Eighteen

If I told you that Forrest not only waited for me but that he *sat with me* on the bus, would you believe it? How is it that the very worst thing and the very best thing could happen to me within the same twenty-minute stretch of time?

"I was trying to tell you before class," Forrest said from the window seat.

Taylor had showed him the tape, he told me, and he knew how embarrassed I would be, how embarrassed everyone in it would be.

"She's trying to prove she deserves to be the anchor this year," he said, as if making excuses for her.

"Well, whatever it takes, I guess."

"I know. It's mean. I told her it was mean, but she said 'that's journalism'."

And then he looked off to the side and smiled a little bit, not a cruel smile, but the flash of a smile that told me how much he liked her. He smiled just thinking about her.

I tried to talk more, but I was afraid I might cry—cry because I was so embarrassed and cry because I was sitting so close to Forrest and I wanted him to stay there forever. I stared ahead at the green vinyl seat and bit my lip. He was quiet for a long while, and then he said, "Can I ask you something?"

I turned to him and watched a lock of beachy brown hair fall over his eyebrow.

If I touched it, what would he do? Slap my hand? Let me?

"Yes, you can ask me something," I said.

"Why were you in your locker?"

How embarrassing. Of course, I knew I shouldn't tell him. At this point, my bent knee was either touching his or the electricity between us was just making it feel that way.

"I can't tell you," I said, leaning in, "but someday soon I will *show* you."

Forrest looked at me quizzically. It was a little like the look Taylor shot at me in her *Gotcha!* tape, but it was so much kinder. Not to overanalyze the look on his face, but I wanted to believe that it said "We're friends, maybe with potential for more."

Nineteen

All weekend, I thought of Forrest and how sweet he was to me and hoped that it was more than him just being a good guy. I wanted to know if he had tried to warn anyone else about *Gotcha!* If it was me and only me, then that surely meant something. I also kept weighing in my head the idea of sneaking him into the Pink Locker Society offices. I did say I would show him, didn't I?

My membership in the PLS is probably the coolest thing about me, so I really wanted him to know. And what an adventure it would be. We'd have a shared secret to tie us together always.

Once inside I could show him how the Web site worked, offer him a snack from the fridge, and tell him how the society mysteriously ceased to exist in the 1970s. Wasn't that a cool mystery to unravel? I saw us chatting together on the couch, and then maybe I would ask him about Taylor and why he was with such a miserable girl. Then maybe he would ask my advice, and I would say, "Why don't you go out with someone who really cares about you?" And then he would figure out that *someone* was me.

Of course, there were problems with my plan. I wasn't supposed to let other people into the office. I could be kicked out of the PLS, which—even though only a handful of people would ever know—would be worse than getting caught climbing out of my locker. I can't imagine the Pink Locker Society going on without me. And I can imagine all too well how angry Piper and Kate would be. Then there was the issue of me finding the courage to actually say that Forrest should be going out with someone else—*ahem*—me. With Forrest I usually stuttered and stammered and backed myself into dumb conversations. Remember the ski lift?

But whether I could find the courage or not, maybe I should be more like Kate and stay on my best behavior. The rules were not to take anyone into the PLS offices or reveal that we were in the PLS. "Your clients—the girls who need help—require a certain amount of discretion and confidentiality," Edith had explained to us.

And what if Forrest told Taylor all about it? Forrest could be trusted, I was sure. But Taylor? No way.

I was tossing and turning all this in my head on the way

into school on Monday when Kate and Piper stopped me dead in my tracks. They pulled me into the back of the empty auditorium.

"Look at this," they said, and opened the pink laptop to reveal the Pink Locker Society Web site. Only now there were pop-up boxes crowding the page. And in the boxes there were comments, mean comments directed at the girls who wrote in to us.

La-ha-loooooooser! Boys will never like you. Good Luck! popped up right next to a question from a girl who was tired of having a small chest. It totally drowned out our kind and thoughtful answer about how puberty happens on its own schedule and that she should like and appreciate the body she has today.

We kept on clicking through, and my stomach started to hurt. Our answer about freckles was paired with a pop-up that read: *Lyssa Madurci, I know it's you. You are like one big freckle, and that ain't cool.*

Poor Lyssa. I had kind of suspected it was her, but I would have never said so.

"This can't be happening," Kate said. "These poor girls."

"Who's going to want to come to our site after this?" Piper said.

The girl who wrote in to say she was in love with her older brother's best friend was not spared either. We gave her our best advice on crushes and suggested she get to know him as a friend. But the pop-up blared: *Boo-hoo-hoo! Older guys like hot girls, so give up!*

"Who would do this?" I asked, my voice shaking a little.

I felt panicked, like that time I was boiling water for spaghetti and accidentally set a dish towel on fire.

"Piper, what do we do?"

Piper shook her head and said she'd have to call the computer woman.

"We have to find out who's doing this to us," she said. "Who would hate the Pink Locker Sociey? We get nothing but fan mail."

"It doesn't matter who, we just have to fix it," Kate said.

For weeks, we'd been finding our way and feeling proud of ourselves for helping girls. Now the day had come for a PLS-SOS. Kate whipped out her red phone and texted:

Emergency!

Twenty

At 1:35, more than a little breathless, Kate and I rushed into the PLS offices. Still weirded out by what we had seen that morning, we overlooked our snacks and ran straight upstairs to answer the ringing phone. Piper and Bet were already there. Funny how Bet chose this particular meeting to attend.

On the line were Anna Hansen, the computer consultant, and Edith, the grandmotherly woman who was our point of contact with the Pinkies.

"Hiya, girls, what's the emergency?" Anna asked.

Piper's words came out in a torrent, explaining what was going on and how we didn't know what to do.

"Someone has hacked into our site and they are saying

such awful things." Piper said. "There are probably a dozen girls crying right now. It's revolting!"

We heard the *click-clacks* of typing as Anna and Edith navigated to www.pinklockersociety.org. Edith gasped.

"Oh, my Lord, what is going on?" Edith said.

"Someone has really pulled a fast one here," Anna said.

"How are they doing this?" Bet asked Anna.

"Hackers hack into Web sites in a buncha ways," Anna said. It's going to take some detective work to figure out how they're gettin' in—and to keep them out."

For a few moments, we just stayed quiet—all of us—waiting for a good idea to come to us. It was Edith who spoke first, and she did so in a quiet voice.

"In the best interests of the Pink Locker Society—its past and future—I have no choice but to shut down the Web site," she said.

"Shut it down?" Kate asked.

"Temporarily, I hope," Edith said.

"Let us see if we can get it fixed first. We can't just give up," Piper said.

"I can get right on it," Anna said. "Best case, we'll have it licked in forty-eight hours."

"Yes, please. We don't want to go out of business," I said, sounding a little desperate.

Again, Edith paused. I could almost feel her kindness through the phone. But she stuck to her decision.

"I'm sorry. There's just too much liability here," she said. "I know you girls have worked so hard and were off to a promising start, but we can't let other girls get hurt. It's not the Pink Locker way.

"Anna, please turn the site off until we can figure out what's going on," Edith said. "I'll call an emergency board meeting to let the other Pinkies know. They will be more disappointed than you girls, if you can believe it."

I couldn't believe any of it.

"Dears, I will be back in touch as soon as it's safe to re-start the site. Stay positive," Edith said.

Just like that, Anna pulled down the entire Pink Locker Society site, and our pink world faded to black.

Twenty-one

id you every worry that by wishing something, you made it come true? Confession: I loved the PLS, but before we were shut down, I had wished that it would slow down just a bit. The weight of everyone's problems was sometimes too much. We received more and more questions each week, and it was tough to answer them—and answer them right—and still keep up with my schoolwork. I had a huge English paper that I hadn't even started. And a ton of geometry proofs to do. Sometimes I turned off my phone so I wouldn't have to be bothered with new alerts from our PLS mailbox. But now, after of few days of never hearing that "Think pink!" ringtone, I felt guilty.

In our downtime, Piper, Kate, and I talked about whether we should try to keep up with the questions, just so we'd be prepared for the moment the site turned back on. But in the end, we decided that made no sense. People asked us questions in the moment, and by the time we were back in business, their problems might have been solved or changed. It wasn't long before I started to miss the PLS. I liked being needed. And I was ready to tackle more questions in my "area of expertise," which turned out to be embarrassing stuff.

So far, I had done especially well with questions about bad breath, stinky feet, and accidentally tooting in class. After the *Gotcha!* incident, I guess I was the school expert on humiliation. Actually, I couldn't have answered these questions without our school nurse, Mrs. Wolff, who must be starting to think I'm a pretty odd girl, to be worried about so many things at once. Somehow it wasn't embarrassing to ask an embarrassing question when it wasn't really about you. It was easy for me to ask questions about periods, for instance, since mine was still totally MIA. On that subject, there was no end to what girls wanted to know: Can you swim with your period? Do periods hurt? Should I eat certain foods during my period? I got answers for every one.

To my positive delight, *Gotcha!* did not appear on MSTV after that first week. Principal Finklestein halted it—at least temporarily—and announced a plan to have a contest for the MSTV Friday-afternoon slot. That didn't mean Taylor was out of the running, just that she had competition. All a student had to do was submit a video.

I thought for a moment about submitting my own video. I would have loved to interview everyone who was embarrassed in Taylor's first episode. But then I thought it would just draw more attention to stuff that everybody, including me, would have preferred to forget. Not that I had any time for another extracurricular activity. Even with the break from the PLS, I was still drowning a bit in my schoolwork, track, and everything else.

Principal Finklestein said we'd see all the videos at a school assembly, where there'd be a panel of judges including him, Ms. Russo, and a couple of real journalists from the local TV station and daily newspaper. We students would have "input" into the final choice, he said. But it was clear the panel would choose the winner.

Ordinarily, I would have been up in arms. After all, it's our TV station; shouldn't we students get to be the final judges? But in this case—suspecting Principal F. was no fan of *Gotcha!*—I was fine with it. In art class, I was happy to hear Ms. Russo say Taylor's broadcast could have been "tweaked" to be more playful and kindhearted. But she also had us debate whether *Gotcha!* was "free speech" and protected by the First Amendment. This only served to annoy me, especially when Taylor pled her own case.

"I have a right to say what I want when I want," she told the class, predicting that she would win again in the end.

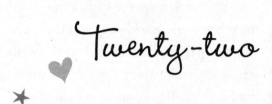

Twenty-two

I know that what I did wasn't right. But the more I thought about the PLS, I thought it might not be so bad to let Forrest in on the secret, especially right now while we were on this forced vacation. Anna said she'd text us when the hackers had been stopped, but forty-eight hours had passed and we still had no idea how long we'd have to wait.

To prepare myself, I wrote a script for exactly what I would say to Forrest about the whole thing. Memorizing my lines made me feel sort of confident. Of course, I had to guess at what he would say back, but I figured I knew him pretty well. After all, did anyone else know that his favorite jelly was the mixed-fruit flavor—the kind you usually find only in those packets at a diner?

I planned it out like a crime and decided that I'd carry

it out on Thursday during my empty study hall period. That morning, I even pretended to worry about where I'd go during study hall, now that there was no reason for us to sneak into the Pink Locker Society offices. It was just depressing to turn on our computers and see all the questions stacking up. Girls were already complaining: "Where are you?" and "Hello? Is anyone home in there?"

Piper and Kate said they were going to spend their study halls in the library.

"Me too," Bet said, quickly adding that she needed to find a spot to study alone.

I said (lied) that I had found an empty classroom in the art and music wing and that I too wanted to be alone to do those geometry proofs. I watched the three of them walk toward the library together and I prepared to spring into action.

My head felt like a balloon filled with love, fog, and electricity. I held my hand out and saw that it was shaking a little. Fortunately, Forrest was easy to capture. He was at his locker, right next to mine, just before study hall started. He often spent his study halls in the gym working out. No one would miss him, I figured. When the hall crowds thinned, I leaned over to Forrest and spoke my first scripted line: "I can *show* you now."

Lesson number one to all you girls out there who really like a boy: Don't count on him remembering everything you ever said to him. You may think you have inside jokes and your own secret code, but you probably don't.

Forrest just looked startled and said, "What?" And when I said it again—"I can show you now"—he said, "What?" again. Maybe I should have started with something like hi.

Anyway, this led to me doing a lot of overexplaining, burbling on about our conversation on the bus and *Gotcha!* and how I said I would *show* him someday and now I was ready to *show* him. Finally, I saw a glimmer of recognition sweep across his face. I looked over my right and left shoulders, then motioned to the inside of my locker.

"What?" he said, but he tipped his head in my direction and looked in.

He squinted as if maybe something was wrong with his vision and took a step back.

"What's in *there*?" he whispered.

I leaned into my locker and worked the combination dial. The combination hadn't changed since the site had been shut down.

"That's what I want to show you," I said as I swung open the pink door. "C'mon."

I went in, and once he saw me standing in there, he followed. He even pulled my locker door closed behind him.

In my script, I was the one who closed the locker door, but no matter. I was having trouble sticking to my script anyway. It wasn't that Forrest said anything so different from what I had guessed he would say. But once we were in the Pink Locker Society offices, he said nothing at all.

Standing there, he looked a little afraid. I think he was mad at me. Later, I had to feel sorry for him. On my first trip into the PLS headquarters, at least I had a little warning and time to get mentally prepared. Forrest just got pulled in, kidnapped almost. His face started to soften after I explained where we were and what this was all about.

"I'm the Pink Locker Society. I mean, I'm *in* the Pink Locker Society. This is our office. You know what the PLS is, right?"

Now Forrest gave me a look of disbelief, but then I pulled him toward the loft to show him the computers. Then I whipsawed back to kitchen area.

"Usually, there are snacks," I said as I grabbed a box of crackers.

"Want some?"

"No," Forrest said—his first word.

"Well, maybe if I had mixed-fruit jelly for the crackers?"

OK, girls. Have you heard me loud and clear? Assume no inside jokes or secret code. After that fruit-jelly remark, he looked at me as if I were wearing my underwear as a hat. Zero recognition. Maybe he had moved on to something more exotic in the jelly department.

I turned and pulled him back up to the loft, where I continued to talk too fast and move too fast. Forrest seemed to wake up when I turned on the computer up in the loft and went to the Web site. Edith had left the home

89

page up. A message apologized for the "temporary inter-ruption."

"Oh, I've seen this," he said. "Taylor goes there all the time."

Great. He's said eleven words to me and one of them was Taylor.

"What's it all about?" he asked.

You can imagine that my answer was a little awkward. I like Forrest *a lot* so I don't exactly want to discuss PBBs with him. I mean, for me, he's the second B, after all. What I did tell him was that girls need to know a lot of stuff as they get older, and the PLS helps them get answers to embarrassing questions.

"Like about growing up, changes, and crushes and stuff," I said.

"Okay, so why did you bring *me* in here?" he asked.

I knew the answer. In fact, I could have answered by describing all the layers of reasons I wanted Forrest to come to this place: to see something that mattered to me, something that made me special, and to see something that finally explained why I was climbing out of my locker in Taylor's *Gotcha!* video. But I never got the chance to speak.

Just then, we heard some noises from across the room. *Ka-chink* went a locker door, and then we saw a shaft of light. Before I could see who it was, Forrest was off down the stairs. I saw him head for my my pink locker door.

I waited just a moment longer, long enough to see Bet land in the room.

"Oh, Jemma. It's you. . . . ," Bet said, looking up to the left and surprised to see me.

Did she see the back of Forrest flying out of there?

"Uh, I have to go," I said, bolting toward my locker door.

I was momentarily crushed inside the locker with Forrest. He was jiggling the latch so frantically, I was worried about the noise coming through on the other side.

"I'll get it. I'll get it," I whispered.

And then I paused just a few seconds before letting us out. I stopped to savor the smell of Forrest's hooded sweatshirt. I inhaled slowly and deeply, and then Forrest said, "Open the door. I'm suffocating." I let out my breath and let him go.

My heart was pounding. After we stepped out of my locker, I wanted to explain that it was just Bet (though I could not explain *why* she was there). I wanted to finally give Forrest my layer cake of reasons why I wanted him to see the sacred offices of the Pink Locker Society. But Forrest quickly gathered his stuff from his own locker and, before I could utter a word, said he had to get going. I wanted a moment more to try to figure out if he was running off because he was worried about getting in trouble, or if he didn't want anyone to see him alone with me. But he didn't give me another moment. He turned, and I could only watch him hustle down the hall, cleats in hand, getting farther and farther away from me.

Twenty-three

One thing I didn't think about was what I would do *after* Forrest and I had our pink locker moment. Fog, electricity, and love still filled my brain like a cloudy mess, but I started to feel more like myself. I wanted to tell Kate and Piper (especially Kate) what had happened. Had I made any progress with him? What did his actions mean, or how might we interpret them? But I had no one to overanalyze with.

I couldn't tell Kate or Piper anything without admitting that I lied. I took Forrest—a boy, no less—behind the pink locker door. I risked the future of the Pink Locker Society, all to make myself look good. It was like in a spy movie and I had become the weak link, blabbing about the secret stuff, endangering our mission. Before all this, I would have bet all the money I have (forty-seven dollars, some of it in quarters) on my belief that Forrest would tell no one. But after a week passed and Forrest had not uttered one word to me about the locker incident, I started to doubt him. Perhaps I had made a terrible mistake, and it would, sooner or later, catch up with me.

It was nearly killing me that I couldn't say anything to anyone about Bet sneaking into the Pink Locker Society offices. I mean, I could have asked her what she was doing in there. But then she might have asked me what *I* was doing in there. And that was a question I really didn't want to answer. I knew that Bet hadn't said anything to anyone so far about my being there, but I didn't know if she was staying quiet out of respect for me or because she didn't want to admit what *she* was up to.

So since I couldn't talk about Forrest or share my suspicions about Bet, I actually got caught up on my schoolwork. I even got an A on my English paper. That gave me something good to tell Mom. But before long, I started to focus less on school and more intently on the uncertain future of the Pink Locker Society. I had a long list of questions and complaints:

- Would Edith and Anna ever get back in touch to say the Web site was working again?
- Was the PLS gone forever?
- What are girls going to do without us?

- We are like doctors, and they have closed the emergency room!
- Who knows how many girls are waiting?!!!!!

I wrote all that down in a note to Kate and Piper that I dashed off during geometry class. I probably shouldn't have been so energetic about those last exclamation points. The pencil tapped loudly against the hard plastic of the desktop: *Line-dot! Line-dot! Line-dot! Line-dot! Line-dot!*

As I finished that last exclamation point, Mr. Ford leaned down and said, "What are you working on, Jemma?"

Great. I'm already annoyed at the whole world and Mr. Ford calls me out for writing notes in class. Worst of all, he took the note.

With the note gone, I grabbed Kate and Piper after class and told them all my complaints about the Pink Locker Society. Turns out, they were getting pretty fed up, too. I don't know if she was just trying to fit in, but Bet chimed in and said she felt "sick in my stomach" thinking about all those girls writing in and getting no response.

"What if people think *we* wrote those nasty notes?" Kate asked.

"They probably do, since we're completely shut down right now," Piper said, then threw up her hands in frustration.

In a quiet voice, Kate said she was so upset that she turned to her mom for advice.

This made all of us turn at look at Kate, because no one had told her mom about the Pink Locker Society. Remember the rules? Tell no one.

"My mom was in the Pink Locker Society," Kate said.

Mrs. Parker?

We exploded with questions for Kate.

- What was it like back then?
- What did they do when there was no Web site?
- Why were we picked?
- Does she have any idea who would hack into the site?
- Are we doing a good job?
- Did she always keep it a secret?
- Why did the Pink Locker Society shut down years ago?
- And who decided it should reopen?
- Can she help us get this junk off of the Web site?

Kate tried to answer them all. Her mother told her it had been a great honor and she loved serving as a Pink Locker Lady. Mrs. Parker confirmed that girls have always wanted to know pretty much the same stuff, Kate said. She also confirmed what Edith had said about how girls used to submit questions through secret boxes hidden around the school.

"Mom said they typed up the answers and published their own little newspaper, *The Pink Paper*. They left stacks of *Pink Papers* in the girls' bathroom," Kate said.

"That's classy," Piper said.

"Well, it makes sense. Girls would find them there," Kate said.

This was all a great history lesson, but Kate's mom had no answers to any of our here-and-now questions about the Pink Locker Society. I could see Piper growing distracted. She picked up her phone and starting checking messages.

"My mom doesn't know why they decided to start it up again," Kate said. "And she doesn't know why they got shut down way back when."

"Sweet!" Piper said, raising her phone up high like it was a trophy she just won.

We looked at her, waiting for the news. I figured it was yet another boy asking her out. They were getting hotter and older with each passing month of eighth grade.

"The Pink Locker Society is back in business," Piper said. "Anna just texted us. The hackers are gone, so let's get to work."

Twenty-four

I should have been happy, and I was. But something about passing through that pink locker door took me back to the last time I was in that office. I could barely concentrate as we waded through more than three hundred questions. We had received on average a hundred per week, even though we were shut down. And one of them, quite obviously, was from Taylor. Grrrrrr.

The message said:

"Hey, secret Pink Locker people, you should SERI-OUSLY consider putting that awesome show Gotcha! *on this Web site!"*

Forrest did tell me Taylor was on our Web site a lot, but

seriously? The Pink Locker Society site will NEVER broadcast *Gotcha!*

I tried to put that out of my mind and dove back into embarrassing issues, starting with someone who was afraid to say she was scared to get braces. I could answer that one easily, having braces myself and knowing that it doesn't hurt to get them on and it's no big deal. But my mind kept drifting, drifting back to Forrest. I started to get really angry that he hadn't said one word to me since that study hall in the PLS. I mean, what was up with that? I showed him something personal and really cool, and he doesn't say anything? I wanted to poke him in the chest and, once and for all, get it on the table: I LIKE YOU FORREST MC-CANN. DON'T YOU GET IT? ARE YOU BLIND?

Ordinarily, Kate would talk me out of such foolishness. But there I was, locked in my own little head, unable to say anything to anyone. Even Piper would have talked sense into me, probably. But no, I forged ahead.

I had no script this time, which turned out to be even more dangerous than having a script. Last time, I at least had the memory of what I wanted to say. This time I was just freestyling when I stopped him by the water fountain.

"Don't you have anything to say to me?"

"Hey, Jemma. What?"

His green eyes were so clear when you got to look at them close. I realized right then that I hardly ever looked him square in the eye. I mean I looked at him from afar, but not straight on like that. I had so much I wanted to say. I wanted to just unravel right there in front of him.

First I said, "Um . . . Um." Then I said the first thing that came to mind:

"I saw someone throw up in that water fountain once."

"Nasty," Forrest said. "It wasn't today, was it?"

Once I said no, he stopped and took a drink. Then he was gone again.

Does it surprise you to learn how, that afternoon, a cold autumn rain poured down over Margaret Simon Middle School? What a perfect match to my mood. It rained extra hard when I was walking home from the bus stop—the kind of rain that gets you even under your umbrella. Thoughts of the restarted PLS Web site cheered me a little. But I couldn't stop thinking of how I had just had an actual encounter with Forrest, and the subject I decided to discuss was puke.

Twenty-five

We truly were back in business. For a few days, we checked the Web site every few hours, like it was a sleeping baby. We wanted to be completely sure that the hackers were gone for good. Anna told us that she had to do a lot of patching, but she felt 95 percent confident that we were in the clear.

"Not one hundred percent?" Edith had asked her on a recent conference call.

We started to answer questions again, and our fan mail resumed. That helped us all to exhale and get back in our Pink Locker groove. During study hall, we answered question after question. And they just kept on coming. We started to think about fair ways of answering questions, if we couldn't answer them all. I suggested a lottery, but Kate thought we should read them all and answer the most urgent ones. In the end, we resolved just to keep doing our best.

But it did not seem to me like we were doing our best on Friday, when Piper and Bet weren't doing any work at all. They bolted in during study hall and scooted upstairs to the loft. I ignored them for a while. But then I started to worry that if Piper and Bet were suddenly best buddies, maybe Bet was up there right now telling Piper about the Forrest incident.

"What are they doing up there?" I finally asked Kate.

"Piper's helping her with her makeup, for the contest. Didn't she tell you?"

"The contest—the MSTV contest?"

"Right. I hope she wins," Kate said.

"Bet's going up against Taylor?"

"Taylor and everyone else who's trying to get their own show," Kate said.

This was an odd development. I wasn't Bet's biggest fan, but I would root for her over Taylor any day.

Piper came bounding down the steps from the loft, holding her big professional-looking makeup case. Bet followed her, walking slowly and wearing a trim navy blue dress. Her eyelashes were curled and her lips were a soft pink.

"I don't know if I can do this," Bet said.

"Sure you can," Kate said.

Twenty-six

Assemblies go one of two ways at Margaret Simon: They're either horribly dull, or everyone gets sooooooooo into it that it's completely rowdy and Principal Finklestein threatens all kinds of punishments until it's over. The anchorperson contest turned out to be one of the wild ones.

It was kind of like a reality TV show where everyone is competing and there's something big at stake. Taylor auditioned first and showed a new round of *Gotcha!* clips, hoping to make an impression on the audience. Thankfully, there was no footage of me this time. Unlike the ones in her first show, these clips seemed very inside-jokey, and sometimes it wasn't clear which part was the "Gotcha!" part. Some of the kids featured didn't go to our school, so they just didn't pack the same punch. Quickly, the audience grew so rowdy you couldn't hear much of what was going on.

The restlessness started to take shape and turned into a chant that began at low volume but rose loud and clear: "Bor-ing! Bor-ing! Bor-ing!" When nearly everyone seemed to be saying it, I joined in, too—after checking around to make sure Forrest wasn't anywhere nearby. I didn't want him to see me being mean.

Principal Finklestein intervened, of course, and when Taylor's segment ended, there was some brief, polite applause. A few people booed, which made me wonder if they would boo for Bet too.

Clem was next. She put a new spin on her old show, *Clem's Crib*. This one was *Around the World with Clem Caritas*. In it, she showed the camera her favorite fashion souvenirs: a batik sarong from Bali, a sickly expensive purse from L.A., some rose soap that "someone really lovely" gave her in Paris. You get the idea. Clem received no boos, and at the end people cheered for her so that her name stretched to two syllables. "Cleh-em! Cleh-em!" But I think they cheered because she was great to look at no matter what she was talking about.

The other entrants received pretty much the same excited response. There was the kid who did magic tricks. Not bad, actually, but it didn't seem like he knew enough tricks to do a weekly show all year long. One girl performed a one-woman play, *Me and My Dog, Sophie*. It was cute and funny, and, afterward, people in the audience shouted "Woof! Woof! Woof!" I thought she might win. A dog in cute little people clothes would be a hard act to follow. Bet was next.

Her video began to roll, and I felt a shiver as I saw images of the Pink Locker Society Web site.

What was she doing—blowing our cover? Is this what she was doing that day I caught her in our office?

My heart was beating so loudly I heard it in my ears— *kunga, kunga, kunga*. The audience was hushed.

"Have you heard of the Pink Locker Society? If you have, I bet you're a girl," Bet told the camera in a serious anchorperson voice.

She went on to say how the Pink Locker Society was performing "a vital service for the young women of Margaret Simon Middle School." Her voice sounded a little thin, but before anyone could shout "Bor-ing!" she asked the audience a question.

"So why would someone vandalize this reputable site with horribly rude comments?"

Bet showed some screen shots of those awful remarks splattered over the Pink Locker site.

"Those of you who frequent the Pink Locker Web site probably have seen these wretched commentaries. To someone who was having body-confidence issues, the hacker wrote 'La-ha-loooooser! Boys will never like you.'"

"Well," Bet said, "I think the hacker is the la-ha-loooooooser. And I'm pleased to say my investigation has uncovered the true identity of this person."

Bet waited—a dramatic pause. I myself was rapt with attention. I shot a look at Piper and Kate, whose eyes were locked on the huge video screen in front of us.

"I was concerned about accusing this person," Bet said, "because a good journalist does not just blindside someone without giving them a chance to speak. For my investigation, I partnered with a very fine computer consultant, and I had a hunch of my own. But what if I was wrong?"

As she spoke, Bet was seated at an anchor desk, her hands neatly folded in front of her. She looked so calm, cool, and collected. I, on the other hand, was at the edge of my seat.

"What I'm about to show you proves that I was not wrong," Bet said. "But before I get to that, my investigation also has uncovered some surprising bits of history about the Pink Locker Society."

OK, under normal circumstances, I'd be very interested in whatever historical odds and ends Bet had dug up. But right this minute? No. Like everyone in the entire auditorium, I wanted to know who it was. Who was the hacker?

"Did you know the PLS mysteriously halted its operations in 1976?" Bet asked.

In her video, she scanned over old copies of *The Pink Paper* on the screen and an open copy of the 1976 Margaret Simon yearbook. We were all waiting, waiting.

"More to come on that in future reports," Bet said finally.

"Back to the hacker who vandalized the Pink Locker Society Web site. It is someone familiar to us all. And, to my great surprise, she freely admitted what she did on camera. She said she was not worried about getting in trouble. She said her comments, which led to the temporary shutdown of the PLS site, were meant to be—her words here—'funny and edgy.' So who is this mystery girl?"

Another generous pause. The entire auditorium watched and waited. Then the screen cut to Taylor Mayweather.

"Yes, I did it," Taylor said, flipping hair over one shoulder. "I saw it as an elegant prank—an extension of my 'Gotcha!' brand and persona. If I want to be a reality TV star, I can't take careful little steps. I have to be bold and daring."

I was stunned—so stunned that I had to remind myself to breathe. *Inhale, exhale,* I told myself.

"But Taylor, what about the girls whose feelings were almost certainly hurt?" Bet asked.

Taylor laughed in an irritated way, like Bet was asking a dumb question.

"I was going to tell everyone it was me as soon as I won the MSTV contest and started my weekly show."

"But again, I have to ask, what about the people you hurt?" Bet asked once more.

"I-I didn't think about *hurting* people. I was just thinking that it would be funny. Totally surprising, don't you think?"

The camera cut back to anchorwoman Bet, who explained that Taylor had enlisted an accomplice. Bet said this accomplice—whom Bet had chosen not to identify—was an accomplished student and computer expert. He figured out how to break into the Pink Locker Society Web site, Bet said, and he gave Taylor the access she needed to make her catty remarks. Immediately, I knew her accomplice had to be Gabe, the sweet geeky guy people said Taylor had been flirting with. The poor guy.

Bet went on to say that Taylor said she wouldn't be hacking into the PLS site any more.

"I've kind of been there, done that, you know what I mean?" Taylor told the camera.

At this point, the entire audience seemed to be scanning the rows of auditorium seats. We were all looking for Taylor. Where was she, and was she really so casual about all this? Surely Principal Finklestein would be whisking her away for some kind of disciplinary hearing.

"It's not for me to say how this 'prank' should be punished," Bet said. "But I'd like to conclude my report by applauding the women—past and present—who are making it a little easier to grow up. Each question the Pink Locker Society answers is a random act of kindness, a lifeboat to someone who feels like they are going under. My only regret is that you guys don't have the same service. Though boys would never admit it, I suspect a Blue Locker Society would be just as popular as the pink one."

With that, her segment ended. Bet had saved the title of her proposed show for the end. She called it *On Your Side? You Bet!* The crowd erupted in, what else? "You Bet! You Bet! You Bet!" They were louder cheers than before. Some people, including Piper, were on their feet. Bet deserved to win. Even I had to admit it. Taylor, on the other hand, should be sent to live alone on some island with just the seagulls to keep her company.

I felt a surge of real happiness when Principal Finkle-stein made it official and called Bet to the stage. Bet took a bow then looked out on the crowd and smiled—not a fake anchorwoman smile, either—a genuine one.

Twenty-seven

I was in a great mood as I walked home from track practice that day. Just a few hours earlier, Bet had won and
Taylor had lost in more ways than one. I wondered what
kind of punishment she would face at school. I had the
urge to get in her face and yell "Gotcha!" but I restrained
myself. Was it too much to hope that she'd be expelled?
But I didn't want Gabe to be kicked out of school. I was
sure he was just another of her victims. And, of course, I
was praying that Bet's dramatic report was all the evidence
Forrest would need to finally break up with Taylor.

Thanks to all that had happened, I was no longer ob-
sessing about my water-fountain incident with Forrest.
Without realizing it, I think I was starting to give myself
the advice that I would have given any other girl. "Let it

go," I would tell her. "He's probably forgotten it by now. Maybe someday he'll like you, too."

My mind wandered the closer I got to home. I thought about how I would burst in the door and tell my mother how my grades had finally started to improve, just in time for report cards. When I had good news, I liked to start out looking very serious and down. (My mother fell for this every time, owing to her natural tendency to imagine the worst possible scenario.) Getting her all concerned first would make it all the more fun to spring the happy news on her. What I really wanted to talk about—with anyone who would listen, even Mom—was Bet's report and the Pink Locker Society. But I knew I couldn't do that.

Two more blocks to go: Thoughts of Forrest always figured into any thoroughly good mood of mine, and this one was no different. I made a bold decision as I crossed Muir Avenue. I decided that the next time I talked to him, I would just try to be normal and relaxed—or as normal and relaxed as I could be. I was not ready to give up my glimmer of hope, my candle in the dark for him. But not knowing how he felt about me was starting to wear me out. Maybe a new low-key script was in order? As I turned the corner on my block, I started playing with opening lines. *Nothing too clever this time*, I promised myself.

But all thoughts of my new script washed away when my house came fully into view. A bunch of cars were clustered in our driveway and lined up along the sidewalk.

You welcome such a sight when you're having a party. But when you're not, you only worry that something is terribly wrong. I broke into a run and didn't stop until I reached my front door. On the way, I passed not just my mother's car but the bike my father rode to his office every day. I moved too fast to catalog the other cars, except one. The green Jeep, I recognized instantly. It belonged to Forrest's mom.

Our lacquered black front door was open, so I pulled on the storm door and stepped into the living room, which was filled with people. Their murmuring conversations stopped when they saw me. They were standing around like they were at a party, but without food or drinks. My mom and dad stepped out of the crowd.

"Jem, there are some . . . um . . . people from school who need to talk with you," Dad said.

I couldn't form a question, but I looked around the room and said words: "School people. Need. Me?"

Then Principal Finklestein came forward. I felt faint seeing him walk through my living room, getting closer and closer until he was standing right in front of me.

"Miss Colwin, we need to ask you about some potentially inappropriate activity."

"What? What do you mean?"

My voice sounded like I was about to cry. My distress only grew when I looked around the room and saw Piper, Kate, and Bet. And their parents.

"This is about the Pink Locker Society, Jemma," Principal Finklestein said.

It sounded so strange to hear those words hit the air in my living room, with so many people standing around to hear them.

"What . . . What about it? Bet did a whole report on it today. Taylor's the one who wrote all that rude stuff."

"He says that's not the point," Piper said.

She was standing against our living room wall, with her arms folded and biting her lower lip.

"What?" I said. "But Taylor admitted it. You heard Bet's report and you picked her as the winner."

I looked around the room for some kind of gesture of support, but all the faces looked blank. They knew more than I did, clearly.

Principal Finklestein put a hand on my shoulder in a fake-seeming gesture of concern.

"Jemma, Bet's winning should not be interpreted as an endorsement of this . . . this unofficial school club," he said. Then he looked around the room seeking nods from the adults.

"I maintain Bet was the most qualified video journalist, but I can't abide what's been happening on this Web site," Prinicpal Finklestein said.

My mom's laptop was open on the coffee table. She sighed out loud and turned the computer screen to where I could see it. Today, we had answered a question from a girl who said she was desperate to have her first kiss but also was worried because her parents said she's too young for a boyfriend.

"This material is simply not appropriate," Principal Finklestein said. "Children can't be dispensing advice to children on these subjects."

He laughed a short, snorty laugh and continued.

"We need to ask you and your friends to stop operating this Web site immediately—or risk suspension from school," Principal Finklestein said.

"What about Taylor? Why don't you punish her?" Piper said.

"I have no way of verifying the veracity of Bet's report and, to be quite honest, I'd rather not dip into that pool. The best thing for all involved would be for our school board—and all our school district's parents—never to hear anything about this. I'd have a riot on my hands."

Again, he laughed that short snort of a laugh.

The next sound I heard was Bet sniffling from our brown leather chair, where she was seated, still in her anchorwoman outfit.

"I'm so sorry, Jemma. He made me tell who all of you were," she said, and dropped her head into her hands.

Kate was sitting on the arm of the chair. She leaned down and patted Bet's back, like your mom might. Kate shot me a look that said "What are we going to do now?"

"He took the laptop," Piper said.

"We had no choice but to seize the instrument that permitted all this to occur," the principal said.

"We were trying to help people," Kate said.

"Right," I said, "and it's Taylor who messed it all up."

The principal responded by saying that while our intentions might have been good, he was concerned with "outcomes" and "liability." Among themselves, the grownup conversation then turned to why, "in this day and age," none of us had told our parents.

Well, not exactly none.

I locked eyes with Kate. Her mother spoke up next.

"I blame myself," Kate's mom told the crowd. "I was a part of this Pink Locker group twenty years ago, and I told her it was okay."

The crowd murmured as if they were trying to figure out if that was terrible or an understandable mistake. Principal Finklestein was the first to speak.

"Maybe it was fine twenty years ago, but not anymore," he said. "Times have changed."

I felt dizzy and sick. No one had mentioned Edith yet, and I sure wasn't going to bring her up. With no real destination in mind, I wove in and around the people in my living room until I was in the kitchen. Then I moved through there into the laundry room.

I opened the extra fridge and thought about getting something to drink. But instead I just stared into the cool air, unable to focus on any one thing. I needed a moment to absorb what had just happened. I needed more than a moment, actually. The secret society we were in had been entirely revealed. And that is why, at 5:25 in the afternoon, my living room was filled with my school principal, my best friends, as well as the boy I am in love with, and everyone's parents.

Because I was still in this state of early absorption, I was not prepared to hear that boy call my name. But he did. Forrest was standing in the door frame of the laundry room and looked a little like he did that day I dragged him into the PLS offices. Not scared exactly, but rattled.

"You all right?"

I studied him for a moment like he was a ghost, probably because I often imagined what it would be like if he were where I was. Last summer, I pictured him on the seat next to mine during that long whale-watching boat tour my family took. I've also imagined him at the other end of the pool as I executed a perfect dive, my painted, pointed toes entering the water with hardly a splash. All that imagining made him seem unreal, but here he was: just a boy in the doorway of my laundry room. He was standing next to the old washboard my mom hung on the wall.

I don't know how much time passed with me just staring at him. But when he repeated his question to me, I just said, "No, I don't think so."

"It's going to be okay," Forrest said. "They told my

mom and me that we're not going to get in any trouble. They just want all this to go away."

Then, like a bucket of cold water, it hit me. Forrest was there, being interrogated along with the rest of us, entirely because of me. I dragged him into this.

"God, they know you were in there, right?" I said. "How? I didn't tell anyone."

Then the second bucket of cold water hit me: Bet had told them about Forrest too.

"Oh," I said, mostly to myself.

"Don't be mad at her. She's freaking out. They probably told her they would kick her out of school if she didn't talk," Forrest said.

Even in the midst of everything, I enjoyed the fact that Forrest had kind of read my mind there. It was then that I shivered and realized I was still holding the refrigerator door open. I turned my back on Forrest and told the water bottles and the extra milk jug that I was sorry.

"What?" Forrest said.

Then I closed the fridge, turned to him, and said it—in English, in person, and out loud.

"I'm so sorry, Forrest, about everything."

Here came the pause I was so worried about. He could say anything or nothing. I held my breath because I didn't want to think about what it would be like to go to school on Monday, and all the other days that would follow, if I couldn't look forward to seeing Forrest there. But he didn't stay silent. And he didn't say he hated me. Or that he didn't want to talk to me ever again.

"It's okay," he said. "And I didn't say anything to Taylor."

"Good," I said. "That's good."

Right then I wanted to ask him if he was going to break up with her. But I just could not do it. Instead, I just stood there staring in his direction.

Then Forrest smiled at me, the smile of old times. He smiled like that when we used to play flashlight tag and that time when we ate pizza at the Fourth of July fireworks. It was back before he was my number-one obsession. Years ago, he was just a boy who was my friend. Maybe that's what he still was, or could be. But before I could analyze our laundry-room moment as much as I wanted to, he said we'd better get going.

Out in the living room, the grown-ups were wrapping up. Principal Finklestein was gone, thankfully, but left a stack of his business cards on the coffee table. Forrest left with his mom. Then one by one, the girls left with their parents until I was left alone with mine. Usually, Mom and Dad want to talk about stuff until the cows come home. But this time they just said, "Why don't you get ready for dinner? It's been a long day."

Never fear, the lecture came soon enough. Later that night, after we ate, my mom and dad told me that I shouldn't have been so secretive. They too said even though we meant well, we shouldn't have gone ahead and started a Web site alone.

"It's too much responsibility, as you unfortunately found out," my mother said.

I wanted to remind them about Taylor and all she had done, but I knew they weren't going to see it exactly my way.

After a little while, I started to cry. I think I cried some for the Pink Locker Society, which now seemed lost forever, like a dream you can only remember bits of. Though it made me seem younger than I am, it felt very good for my parents to be sitting there with me, wiping my tears away and saying what my mother always says: "This too shall pass."

Twenty-eight

It took more than a month, but I started to think less and less about the Pink Locker Society. My grades improved. Piper, Kate, and I were still best friends. We all supported Bet's new MSTV show, but she did not do any further reports about the Pink Locker Society. I remained on the track team, started putting more effort into my running, and seemed to be good at it.

Taylor never did get any kind of school suspension or anything. She and Forrest continued to be a couple, which broke my heart and confused me deeply. Kate was kind enough not to say "I told you so." My mother, quoting Forrest's mom, gave me the only clue I have about the Forrest-Taylor situation. Turns out that the night Principal

Finklestein came over, Mom and Mrs. McCann actually talked about it.

"Vera thinks it's a bit soon for Forrest to have a girl-friend," Mom told me. "But she says something about Tay-lor just fascinates him."

Occasionally, I would hear that recycled rumor about Taylor and Gabe, but it no longer gave me any hope. I knew the story behind the story. I used to take any oppor-tunity to look at Taylor, to check out her clothes and her shoes. But now I just looked the other way whenever she came into view.

What else do you need to know? No, I still hadn't got-ten my period. But I wasn't completely a Flatty McFlat Chest anymore. And, no, I wasn't stuffing my bra.

We didn't know what to do about the pink locker doors. No one ever asked us about Edith, the other Pinkies, or our secret offices. So we assumed nobody knew about that. The hardest part though was not being there for girls who needed us. Sometimes I would run across a sixth-grade girl who looked particularly confused and think that she really needed the Pink Locker Society. I didn't even have to hear her speak to know that she could use some guidance, prob-ably because not so long ago I was that girl. You know the one? She pushes with all her might on the door that says "PULL" in letters as big as her head.

But who would answer her now? Our laptop was gone. The Web site was gone. It had been weeks since our cell phones alerted us to a new question. There might be a thousand questions waiting for us. We didn't know.

School life readjusted to a different rhythm. I wasn't as busy. It felt OK to go at a slower pace, but I missed the work of the Pink Locker Society. It made me feel needed and smart. I learned a lot, including that I wasn't such a freak myself with all my many concerns.

I missed getting thank you letters from our . . . whatever they were . . . our customers, our clients, our friends? Who doesn't like a heap of praise? Not that I need applause all day long, but they always put a smile on my face. I forwarded one of them to my phone and I refused to delete it. It said:

"I thank you soooooooo much for creating this Web site. It makes me feel normal and special at the same time."

The Pink Locker Society did the same for me. And now, I just felt normal. Normal is OK, but it's a wee bit dull. That's why I invited Kate and Piper to my house for a sleepover.

"Viva la sleepovers!" Piper called out when I invited her on Thursday. She sometimes did this—took a phrase and tried to work it into every possible situation. One summer she talked like a pirate from the time school let out until it started up again in August. But now she was on a Spanish kick. So instead of "Long live sleepovers!" or "Woo-hoo

sleepovers!" Piper gave us "*Viva la* sleepovers!" I had to agree. May they never end!

We decided this sleepover should start right after school on Friday, so Piper and Kate walked home from school with me. The night stretched out ahead of us with good stuff planned: a movie, pizza, and then some joint decision making about yearbook photos.

"*Viva la* doorbells!" Piper yelled when the doorbell rang at my house.

The mailman was standing there with a large manilla envelope—the kind with Bubble Wrap lining the inside. It was addressed to my mother, and it was from Margaret Simon Middle School. It was way too heavy to be just a letter.

We found my mother on the sunporch, with her reading glasses on the tip of her nose and a book in her lap. Good old Mom.

She pulled the zip tab on the envelope and pulled out our pink laptop. We shrieked.

"Girls, girls," she said, "let me see what this is all about."

There was a letter taped to the top. Mom read it aloud.

"Dear Mrs. Colwin, Due to the unfortunate events, blah-blah-blah. Our school attorneys tell me it would be inappropriate for me to seize this piece of personal property. Blah-blah-blah. We are returning this laptop in the hope that the girls will use it only for productive purposes. Sincerely yours, Prinicpal Finklestein."

"*Viva la* U.S. Mail!" Piper yelled out.

My mother giggled and said, "Okay, girls. Looks like you can have this computer back. Where did it come from, anyway?"

"It was mine," Piper said, "Thanks."

She grabbed the laptop and we followed her back to the family room.

"*Viva la* laptop!" Piper whispered when we were out of my mother's earshot.

It was just a cold piece of plastic technology, but having the computer back sent us on a trip down memory lane.

"Remember our first meeting when Jem couldn't open the pink locker?" Piper said.

"And remember when Jem decided that Forrest needed a personal tour?" Kate said.

In the weeks since we'd been permanently shut down, I had confessed my wrongdoing.

"Hey, does anyone remember that we actually did some good?" I said. "People loved us. We had fans."

"Let's turn it on," Piper said, "just for old time's sake."

"It's just a computer now. It's nice to have, but not that special anymore," I said.

"Let's see if there's anything left," Piper said, and spun the laptop toward her.

"What must Edith think?" Kate said, "We should have sent her a PLS-SOS."

"And say what? That we've been banned?" Piper said.

Piper clicked around and found that the site was still there. But it was frozen in time, still showing that message about being temporarily shut down.

Meanwhile, between bites of pizza, Kate and I kept talking about all that had happened.

"If you could go back in time, would you do anything differently? Like maybe never step through the pink locker door?" Kate asked me.

"No, I think I'd still go. Well, I'd still go if you pulled me in."

"Oh, my gosh, remember the snacks?" Kate said.

"*Viva la* snacks!" said Piper, pumping a fist in the air and then getting back to her clicking and clacking. Then we heard the laptop start humming; its internal fan started whirring, and simultaneously all three of our phones sprang to life. The old "Think pink!" ringtone. We had messages—Pink Locker Society messages!

"It's probably just Piper cranking us," Kate said.

"Yeah, Pipes. That's cruel. You got us all excited," I said.

"*Viva la* text messages!" Piper said. "Look for yourselves."

She spun the laptop toward Kate and me and we saw it was true. Piper, the computer whiz, had linked us back into our Pink Locker Society mailbox, and we now had dozens of unread text messages. Most of them came in more than a month ago, before news started to trickle out that the site was down, apparently forever. We wanted to read each and every one.

My best friend stole my boyfriend. What do I do?

Can I go on vacation while I have my period?

People tease me because I don't wear makeup. What should I do?

I have a huge crush on my teacher. Help!

I do not have pretty feet. Should I wear sandals anyway?

I'm the shortest girl in my class, and I'm sick of the nicknames. What should I do?

Everyone tells me I look fine, but I still feel fat. How can I lose weight?

On and on they went, a rainbow of woes. Each one represented a person's sincere question. Some were serious issues, others more minor, but each one mattered to someone.

"Gosh, this stinks that we can't answer any of them," Kate said. "We've just abandoned them."

"Look how the number of messages trailed off in the last few weeks. They're forgetting about us," I said.

"Read this one," Piper said.

Hey, are you guys on vacation or something? I wrote twice and the Web site isn't working. It's kind of important. My parents are getting a divorce.

The more messages we read, the more our group mood took a plunge. We had started out all silly and happy. Just moments ago, Piper was shouting, "*Viva la* erasable pens!" and "*Viva la* flannel pajamas!" Now, at least twenty minutes had gone by without a "*Viva la*" anything.

Instead, we kept murmuring at each other about how there was nothing we could do. What could we do? The Pink Locker Society was closed, by order of the principal.

Or was it?

I looked at Kate. Kate looked at Piper, and the two of them looked back at me.

"Nobody said we had to stop helping people," I said.

"Riiiiiight," Kate said, nodding slowly.

It was one of those cosmic friend moments. Silently, we were sharing the same thought—once again three flowers on the same stem. Piper stopped tapping on the keyboard. Kate held her triangle of pizza aloft on the palm of her hand. Sure, none of us knew exactly *how* we would do it. Not yet, anyway.

But I knew what needed to be said. I, Jemma, jumped up on the couch and shouted it before Piper could beat me to it: "*Viva la* **Pink Locker Society!**"

Viva La Pink Locker Society!

Now that you're a part of the club,
stay in the pink at

PinkLockerSociety.org.

It's fun and free, so bring your BFF!
Ask questions and get answers.
Decorate your dream locker, make purses,
wish necklaces, and other creative crafts.
Try new recipes, give your opinion,
start a book club*, and *more*!
Find the Pink Locker Society on Facebook, too,
if you're thirteen or older.

*See next page for tips on starting a book club.

Start Your Own Book Club!

Everything is more fun with a friend, including reading a book. That's the whole idea behind book clubs. A group of friends read the same book, talk about it, and snack. What could be better than that?

Follow these steps to start your own book group.

1. Get the word out. Round up four to twelve friends who like to read.
2. Schedule meeting dates. It's important to space your meetings far enough apart that members have enough time to read the books. Many clubs find that a monthly meeting works well, and that keeping it on the same day (such as the first Wednesday of every month) helps.

3. Pick a place. Most clubs take turns meeting at some-one's house, but they can really happen anywhere: after school in an empty classroom, at the public library, or even the local bookstore.
4. Plan for snacks. What fun would a club be without snacks? For variety, ask two or three people to bring some munchies to each meeting.
5. Choose the books. The most important thing! Decide how your group will pick the books. Some groups take turns letting each member choose. Others open it up to the group to decide.

Happy reading!

THE PINK LOCKER SOCIETY

Questions & Answers

The PLS has answers! In this special bonus section, get their trusted advice on dozens of issues. And if you have a question of your own, visit www.pinklockersociety.org to submit it!

Dear PLS,

I have a problem in the boob department. One's bigger than the other. Help!
Lopsided

Dear Lopsided,

Relax! Girls grow a lot during these years and it's common for one breast to get ahead of the other. This usually evens out over time and you are probably the only one who has noticed this small imbalance in your bra. Speaking of bras, as you get older, if you are still a little uneven, you can always use padding on one side.

Think pink!

Dear PLS,

Brown is the most boring color ever created. And it's the color of my boring hair. I want to dye it red or, possibly, pink, but my mom says no. How old do you have to be to dye your hair?

Down With Brown

Dear D. W. B.,

Changing your hair is a fun way to experiment with your look, but the people we asked said girls in middle school shouldn't mess with their hair color. Dyeing your hair means using chemicals on it. Some people report a burning or itching scalp—or even hair loss—after getting their hair dyed. But that aside, we think brown hair is nice. Is yours more golden brown, or a darker brown like deep, dark chocolate? Instead of dyeing it, we'd recommend a new headband, haircut, or hairstyle.

Think Pink! (But not pink hair!)

Hey,

This is going to sound weird, but my boobs are ruining

my life. They are ENORMOOSE boobs. Biggest in the whole school. What do I do?
Signed,
E. B.

Dear E. B,

We hear you! Though lots of girls wish for bigger breasts, when you feel yours are too big, it is no fun. They always seem to get in the way. The best approach is to manage them. Here are good steps to take:

1. Buy bras that fit you well. Go to a store that has someone who can measure and fit you for a bra. This may sound embarrassing, but it's worth it to get a bra that fits right and feels good. If there's no expert fitter, ask your mom, aunt, big sister, or a female friend to help. Also buy a sports bra so you feel comfortable when it's time for gym class or sports.

2. Choose clothes that work with your figure. A good bra will help you wear most any shirt you like, but if you're self-conscious, try not to wear shirts that are too tight or too revealing. You can do a quick check at home to see if your shirt is too revealing. Stand in front of a mirror and bend forward. Your shirt shouldn't open or gap too much.

3. Learn to handle gawkers. It's annoying to have people stare at your chest. But you never have to just put up with rude stares or comments. Tell a parent, teacher, or another adult if someone is bothering you in this way. You can ignore them and walk away, but if you are feeling bold just tell the offending gawker, "Yo, my eyes are up here!"

Think pink!

Dear PLS,

My grandma has breast cancer. I'm very worried about her. Why does this have to happen?
Grandma's Girl

Dear G. G.,

We're sorry to hear about your grandma. We love our grandmothers like no one else in the world. Even experts don't know exactly why someone gets breast cancer, but being older and having a history of it in the family can make a woman more likely to get it. Fortunately, doctors do know a lot about how to fight it. You can be helpful to your grandma by encouraging her during the treatments she is getting to fight the disease. You might consider wearing a pink ribbon or raising money for breast cancer research. A positive attitude can help your grandma—and you.

Think pink!

Dear PLS,

OK, here's a problem for you. I accidentally tooted in class and everyone knows it was me. Now they're calling me Miss Farts A Lot!
Your friend,
Miss You Know What

Dear Miss Y. K. W.,

Oh, dear. That's not a nickname anyone would want. But the truth is that everyone passes gas because everyone digests food. Of course, we'd rather not do it in public, but it happens. If you find yourself feeling gassy again, go to the bathroom or find an out-of-the-way spot. Our guess is that your nickname will eventually fade away. If someone teases you about it in the meantime, remind him or her that everybody toots!

Think pink!

Dear PLS,

Can I swim when I have my period? If so, won't people see the pad in my bathing suit?
Signed,
Super Swimmer

Dear S. S.,

Yes, you can swim when you have your period.

Getting exercise is fun and healthy, so you don't want to avoid something you love. But a girl should wear a tampon to swim. Like a pad, a tampon absorbs the menstrual flow, but it does so from inside the vagina. A tampon is made of absorbent material that is pressed into a cylinder shape. Learning to insert a tampon takes a little practice, but just relax and be patient. Talk to your mom, sister, or someone else who has experience using tampons. Read the directions in the package and remember to change it every four to six hours.

Think pink!

Dear PLS,

My backpack is very heavy. It's like carrying rocks to school every day. How can I get my teachers to give me less homework?
Sincerely,
Weighed Down

Dear W. D.,

This one was a toughie. After about two seconds of discussion, we realized that teachers were not going to ease up on the homework. So the only other solution is to carry less weight and carry it in a way that doesn't hurt your back. We hope these tips lighten your load!

1. Take stock of what's in your backpack and figure

out if you need every item and book in there. We sometimes find balled-up sweatshirts, bits of long-ago lunches, and lots of pennies and nickels swimming in the depths of our backpacks.

2. Use both shoulder straps. We have been guilty of just using one, but two balances the load.

3. Do wheelies! Consider a rolling backpack so you can roll it instead of haul it on your back.

Think pink!

Dear PLS,

I know this is a Web site for girls, but I'm a guy. Here's my question: All the guys I know like the same girl. It makes me mad because I've liked her the longest. How can I tell those guys to back off?

Signed,

A Guy

Dear A. G.,

We're happy to know that guys like our Web site, too. Everyone is welcome here! But back to your question. It stinks when too many people—especially friends—like the same person. In some ways, it's like in soccer or basketball when everyone is fighting for the ball. Hey, that's mine. Give it here! But a girl (or a guy) isn't a piece of sporting equipment. People aren't property, so there's no sense telling other guys they shouldn't like "your" girl. But you can tell this girl that you like her and see what happens. Even though you liked her first, it's up to her to decide whom she likes. Maybe she likes you, too. But be kind if she just wants to be friends.

Think pink (or blue)!

KidsHealth
from Nemours

Every year more than 150 million families, educators, health professionals, and media turn to KidsHealth.org for expert answers, making it the #1 Web site devoted to children's health and development. KidsHealth is physician-led, providing doctor-approved health information about the physical, emotional, and behavioral health of children, from before birth through adolescence. Kids Health.org features three distinct sections—for parents, for kids, and for teens—each with its own tone and age-appropriate topics.

KidsHealth is known for its engaging, family-friendly information and has been honored as one of the 30 Best Web sites by *U.S. News & World Report*, one of the 50 Coolest Web Sites by *Time* magazine, and the Best Family Health Site For Moms by *Good Housekeeping*. KidsHealth also created KidsHealth in the Classroom, a free Web site for educators featuring standards-based health curricula, activities, and handouts.

KidsHealth comes from Nemours, one of the nation's largest nonprofit pediatric health systems and a founding member of the Partnership for a Healthier America, a national movement led by First Lady Michelle Obama to solve the childhood obesity challenge. For more information about KidsHealth, please visit KidsHealth.org.

Tarquin Cardona

About the Author

Debra Moffitt lives in a house full of boys—with three sons and one husband. She was a newspaper reporter for more than ten years and is now the kids' editor of KidsHealth.org. That means she gets paid to write about stuff kids care about, like pimples, crushes, and puberty. She'd like to thank the thousands of girls who have e-mailed her to share their questions and concerns. You inspired this book series!